EX L

VINTAGE CLASSICS

PICTURES OF FIDELMAN

Bernard Malamud, one of America's most important novelists and short-story writers, was born in Brooklyn in 1914. He took his B.A. degree at the City College of New York and his M.A. at Colombia University. From 1940 to 1949 he taught in various New York schools, and then joined the staff of Oregon State University, where he stayed until 1961. Thereafter, he taught at Bennington State College, Vermont.

His remarkable and uncharacteristic first novel, *The Natural*, appeared in 1952. Malamud received international acclaim with the publication of *The Assistant* (1957, winner of the Rosenthal Award and the Daroff Memorial Award). His other works include *The Magic Barrel* (1958, winner of the National Book Award), *Idiots First* (1963, short stories), *The Fixer* (1966, winner of a second National Book Award and a Pulitzer Prize), *Pictures of Fidelman* (1969), *The Tenants* (1971), *Rembrandt's Hat* (1973, short stories), *Dubin's Lives* (1979) and *God's Grace* (1982). Bernard Malamud was made a member of the National Institute of Arts and Letters, USA, in 1964, a member of the American Academy of Arts and Sciences in 1967, and won a major Italian award, the Premio Mondello, in 1985.

Bernard Malamud died in 1986.

ALSO BY BERNARD MALAMUD

The Natural
The Assistant
The Tenants
A New Life
The Magic Barrel
Idiots First
The Fixer
Rembrandt's Hat
Dubin's Lives
God's Grace
The People
The Complete Stories

BERNARD MALAMUD

Pictures of Fidelman

An Exhibition

VINTAGE BOOKS
London

Published by Vintage 2002

4 6 8 10 9 7 5

Copyright © Bernard Malamud 1958, 1962, 1968, 1969

Bernard Malamud has asserted his right under the Copyright, Designs
and Patents Act 1988 to be identified as the author of this work

First published in Great Britain by Eyre & Spottiswode in 1969

Vintage
Random House, 20 Vauxhall Bridge Road,
London SW1V 2SA

www.vintage-books.co.uk

Addresses for companies within The Random House Group Limited
can be found at: www.randomhouse.co.uk/offices.htm

The Random House Group Limited Reg. No. 954009

A CIP catalogue record for this book
is available from the British Library

ISBN 9780099433453

The Random House Group Limited supports the Forest Stewardship
Council® (FSC®), the leading international forest-certification
organisation. Our books carrying the FSC label are printed on FSC®-
certified paper. FSC is the only forest-certification scheme supported
by the leading environmental organisations, including Greenpeace.
Our paper procurement policy can be found at:
www.randomhouse.co.uk/environment

Printed and bound in Great Britain by Clays Ltd, St Ives plc

Not to understand. Yes, that was my whole occupation during those years – I can assure you, it was not an easy one.

Rainer Maria Rilke

The intellect of man is forced to choose
Perfection of the life, or of the work . . .

W. B. Yeats

Both.

A. Fidelman

an exhibition

1

Fidelman, a self-confessed failure as a painter, came to Italy to prepare a critical study of Giotto, the opening chapter of which he had carried across the ocean in a new pigskin leather brief-case, now gripped in his perspiring hand. Also new were his gum-soled oxblood shoes, a tweed suit he had on despite the late-September sun slanting hot in the Roman sky, although there was a lighter one in his bag; and a dacron shirt and set of cotton-dacron underwear, good for quick and easy washing for the traveller. His suitcase, a bulky two-strapped affair which embarrassed him slightly, he had borrowed from his sister Bessie. He planned, if he had any funds left at the end of the year, to buy a new one in Florence. Although he had been in not much of a mood when he had left the U.S.A., Fidelman picked up in Naples, and at the moment, as he stood in front of the Rome railway station, after twenty minutes still absorbed in his first sight of the Eternal City, he was conscious of a certain exaltation that devolved on him after he had discovered directly across the many-vehicled piazza stood the remains of the Baths of Diocletian. Fidelman remembered having read that Michelangelo had helped in converting the baths into a church and convent, the latter ultimately changed into the museum that presently was there. 'Imagine,' he muttered. 'Imagine all that history.'

In the midst of his imagining, Fidelman experienced the sensation of suddenly seeing himself as he was, to the pin-point, outside and in, not without bittersweet pleasure; and as the well-known image of his face rose before him he was taken by the depth of pure feeling in his eyes, slightly mag-nified by glasses, and the sensitivity of his elongated nostrils and often tremulous lips, nose divided from lips by a mous-tache of recent vintage that looked, Fidelman thought, as if it had been sculptured there, adding to his dignified appear-ance although he was a little on the short side. Almost at the same moment, this unexpectedly intense sense of his being – it was more than appearance – faded, exaltation having gone where exaltation goes, and Fidelman became aware that there was an exterior source to the strange, almost tri-dimensional reflection of himself he had felt as well as seen. Behind him, a short distance to the right, he had no-ticed a stranger – give a skeleton a couple of pounds – loitering near a bronze statue on a stone pedestal of the heavy-dugged Etruscan wolf suckling the infant Romulus and Remus, the man contemplating Fidelman already acquisitively so as to suggest to the traveller that he had been mirrored (lock, stock, barrel) in the other's gaze for some time, perhaps since he had stepped off the train. Casu-ally studying him though pretending no, Fidelman beheld a person of about his own height, oddly dressed in brown knickerbockers and black knee-length woollen socks drawn up over slightly bowed, broomstick legs, these grounded in small porous pointed shoes. His yellowed shirt was open at the gaunt throat, both sleeves rolled up over skinny, hairy arms. The stranger's high forehead was bronzed, his black hair thick behind small ears, the dark close-shaven beard tight on the face; his experienced nose was weighted at the tip, and the soft brown eyes, above all, wanted. Though his expression suggested humility he all but licked his lips as he approached the ex-painter.

'Shalom,' he greeted Fidelman.

'Shalom,' the other hesitantly replied, uttering the word – so far as he recalled – for the first time in his life. My God, he thought, a handout for sure. My first hello in Rome and it has to be a schnorrer.

The stranger extended a smiling hand. 'Susskind,' he said, 'Shimon Susskind.'

'Arthur Fidelman.' Transferring his brief-case to under his left arm while standing astride the big suitcase he shook hands with Susskind. A blue-smocked porter came by, glanced at Fidelman's bag, looked at him, then walked away.

Whether he knew it or not Susskind was rubbing his palms contemplatively together.

'Parla italiano?'

'Not with ease, although I read it fluently. You might say I need the practice.'

'Yiddish?'

'I express myself best in English.'

'Let it be English then.' Susskind spoke with a slight British intonation. 'I knew you were Jewish,' he said, 'the minute my eyes saw you.'

Fidelman chose to ignore the remark. 'Where did you pick up your knowledge of English?'

'In Israel.'

Israel interested Fidelman. 'You live there?'

'Once, not now,' Susskind answered vaguely. He seemed suddenly bored.

'How so?'

Susskind twitched a shoulder. 'Too much heavy labour for a man of my modest health. Also I couldn't stand the suspense.'

Fidelman nodded.

'Furthermore, the desert air makes me constipated. In Rome I am lighthearted.'

'A Jewish refugee from Israel, no less,' Fidelman said with good humour.

'I'm always running,' Susskind answered mirthlessly. If he was lighthearted he had yet to show it.

'Where else from, if I may ask?'

'Where else but Germany, Hungary, Poland? Where not?'

'Ah, that's so long ago.' Fidelman then noticed the grey in the man's hair. 'Well, I'd better be going.' He picked up his bag as two porters hovered uncertainly near by.

But Susskind offered certain services. 'You got a hotel?'

'All picked and reserved.'

'How long are you staying?'

What business is it of his? However, Fidelman courteously replied, 'Two weeks in Rome, the rest of the year in Florence, with a few side trips to Siena, Assisi, Padua and maybe also Venice.'

'You wish a guide in Rome?'

'Are you a guide?'

'Why not?'

'No,' said Fidelman. 'I'll look as I go along to museums, libraries, et cetera.'

This caught Susskind's attention. 'What are you, a professor?'

Fidelman couldn't help blushing. 'Not exactly, really just a student.'

'From which institution?'

He coughed a little. 'By that I mean professional student, you might say. Call me Trofimov, from Chekhov. If there's something to learn I want to learn it.'

'You have some kind of a project?' the other persisted. 'A grant?'

'No grant. My money is hard earned. I worked and saved a long time to take a year in Italy. I made certain sacrifices. As for a project, I'm writing on the painter Giotto. He was one of the most important —'

'You don't have to tell me about Giotto,' Susskind interrupted with a little smile.

'You've studied his work?'

'Who doesn't know Giotto?'

'That's interesting to me,' said Fidelman, secretly irritated. 'How do you happen to know him?'

'How do you?'

'I've given a good deal of time and study to his work.'

'So I know him too.'

I'd better get this over with before it begins to amount up to something, Fidelman thought. He set down his bag and fished with a finger in his leather coin purse. The two porters watched with interest, one taking a sandwich out of his pocket, unwrapping the newspaper and beginning to eat.

'This is for yourself,' Fidelman said.

Susskind hardly glanced at the coin as he let it drop into his trouser pocket. The porters then left.

The refugee had an odd way of standing motionless, like a cigar store Indian about to burst into flight. 'In your luggage,' he said vaguely, 'would you maybe have a suit you can't use? I could use a suit.'

At last he comes to the point. Fidelman, though annoyed, controlled himself. 'All I have is a change from the one you now see me wearing. Don't get the wrong idea about me, Mr Susskind. I'm not rich. In fact I'm poor. Don't let a few new clothes deceive you. I owe my sister money for them.'

Susskind glanced down at his shabby baggy knicker-bockers. 'I haven't had a suit for years. The one I was wearing when I ran away from Germany, fell apart. One day I was walking around naked.'

'Isn't there a welfare organization that could help you out – some group in the Jewish community, interested in refugees?'

'The Jewish organizations wish to give me what they wish, not what I wish,' Susskind replied bitterly. 'The only thing they offer me is a ticket back to Israel.'

'Why don't you take it?'

'I told you already, here I feel free.'

'Freedom is a relative term.'

'Don't tell me about freedom.'

He knows all about that too, Fidelman thought. 'So you feel free,' he said, 'but how do you live?'

Susskind coughed, a brutal cough.

Fidelman was about to say something more on the subject of freedom but left it unsaid. Jesus, I'll be saddled with him all day if I don't watch out.

'I'd better be getting off to the hotel.' He bent again for his bag.

Susskind touched him on the shoulder and when Fidelman exasperatedly straightened up, the half dollar he had given the man was staring him in the eye.

'On this we both lose money.'

'How do you mean?'

'Today the lira sells six twenty-three on the dollar, but for specie they only give you five hundred.'

'In that case give it here and I'll let you have a dollar.' From his billfold Fidelman quickly extracted a crisp bill and handed it to the refugee.

'Not more?' Susskind sighed.

'Not more,' the student answered emphatically.

'Maybe you would like to see Diocletian's bath? There are some enjoyable Roman coffins inside. I will guide you for another dollar.'

'No, thanks.' Fidelman said good-bye, and lifting the suitcase, lugged it to the kerb. A porter appeared and the student, after some hesitation, let him carry it towards the line of small dark-green taxis on the piazza. The porter offered to carry the brief-case too but Fidelman wouldn't part with it. He gave the cab driver the address of the hotel, and the taxi took off with a lurch. Fidelman at last relaxed. Susskind, he noticed, had disappeared. Gone with his breeze, he thought. But on the way to the hotel he had an uneasy feeling that the refugee, crouched low, might be clinging to the little tyre on the back of the cab; however he didn't look out to see.

Fidelman had reserved a room in an inexpensive hotel not far from the station with its very convenient bus terminal. Then, as was his habit, he got himself quickly and tightly organized. He was always concerned with not wasting time, as if it were his only wealth – not true, of course, though Fidelman admitted he was an ambitious person – and he soon arranged a schedule that made the most of his working hours. Mornings he usually visited the Italian libraries, searching their catalogues and archives, read in poor light, and made profuse notes. He napped for an hour after lunch, then at four, when the churches and museums were reopening, hurried off to them with lists of frescoes and paintings he must see. He was anxious to get to Florence, at the same time a little unhappy at all he would not have time to take in in Rome. Fidelman promised himself to return if he could afford it, perhaps in the spring, and look at everything he pleased.

After dark he managed to unwind himself and relax. He ate as the Romans did, late, enjoyed a half litre of white wine and smoked a cigarette. Afterwards he liked to wander – especially in the old sections near the Tiber. He had read that here, under his feet, were the ruins of Ancient Rome. It was an inspiring business, he, Arthur Fidelman, after all, born a Bronx boy, walking around in all this history. History was mysterious, the remembrance of things unknown, in a way burdensome, in a way a sensuous experience. It uplifted and depressed, why he did not know except that it excited his thoughts more than he thought good for him. This kind of excitement was all right up to a point, perfect maybe for a creative artist, but less so for a critic. A critic ought to live on beans. He walked for miles along the winding Tiber, gazing at the star-strewn skies. Once, after a couple of days in the Vatican Museum, he saw flights of angels – gold, blue, white – intermingled in the sky. 'My God, I got to stop using my eyes so much,' Fidelman said to himself. But back in his room he sometimes wrote till morning.

Late one night, about a week after his arrival in Rome, as Fidelman was writing a few notes on the Byzantine style mosaics he had seen during the day, there was a knock on the door, and though the student, immersed in his work, was not conscious he had said 'Avanti,' he must have, for the door opened, and instead of an angel, in came Susskind in his shirt and baggy knickerbockers.

Fidelman, who had all but forgotten the refugee, certainly never thought of him, half rose in astonishment. 'Susskind,' he exclaimed, 'how did you get in here?'

Susskind for a moment stood motionless, then answered with a weary smile, 'I'll tell you the truth, I know the clerk.'

'But how did you know where I live?'

'I saw you walking in the street so I followed you.'

'You mean you saw me accidentally?'

'How else? Did you leave me your address?'

Fidelman resumed his seat. 'What can I do for you, Susskind?' He spoke grimly.

The refugee cleared his throat. 'Professor, the days are warm but the nights are cold. You see how I go around naked.' He held forth bluish arms, goosefleshed. 'I came to ask you to reconsider about giving away your old suit.'

'And who says it's an old suit?' Fidelman's voice thickened.

'One suit is new, so the other's old.'

'Not precisely. I am afraid I have no suit for you, Susskind. The one I presently have hanging in the closet is a little more than a year old and I can't afford to give it away. Besides, it's gabardine, more like a summer suit.'

'On me it will be for all seasons.'

After a moment's reflection, Fidelman drew out his billfold and counted four single dollars. These he handed to Susskind.

'Buy yourself a warm sweater.'

Susskind also counted the money, bill for bill. 'If four,' he said, 'then why not five?'

Fidelman flushed. The man's warped nerve. 'Because I happen to have four available,' he answered. 'That's twenty-five hundred lire. You should be able to buy a warm sweater and have something left over besides.'

'I need a suit,' Susskind said. 'The days are warm but the nights are cold.' He rubbed his arms. 'What else I need I won't say.'

'At least roll down your sleeves if you're so cold.'

'That won't help me.'

'Listen, Susskind,' Fidelman said gently, 'I would gladly give you the suit if I could afford to, but I can't. I have barely enough money to squeeze out a year for myself here. I've already told you I am indebted to my sister. Why don't you try to get yourself a job somewhere, no matter how menial? I'm sure that in a short time you'll work yourself up into a decent position.'

'A job, he says,' Susskind muttered gloomily. 'Do you know what it means to get a job in Italy? Who will give me a job?'

'Who gives anybody a job? They have to go out and get it.'

'You don't understand, professor. I am an Israeli citizen and this means I can only work for an Israeli company. How many Israeli companies are there here? – maybe two, El Al and Zim, and even if they had a job, they wouldn't give it to me because I have lost my passport. I would be better off now if I were stateless. A stateless person shows his *laissez-passer* and sometimes he can find a small job.'

'But if you lost your passport why didn't you put in for a duplicate?'

'I did but did they give it to me?'

'Why not?'

'Why not? They say I sold it.'

'Had they reason to think so?'

'I swear to you somebody stole it.'

'Under such circumstances,' Fidelman asked, 'how do you live?'

'How do I live?' He chomped with his teeth. 'I eat air.'

'Seriously?'

'Seriously – on air. I also peddle,' he confessed, 'but to peddle you need a licence and that the Italians won't give me. When they caught me peddling I was interned for six months in a work camp.'

'Didn't they attempt to deport you?'

'They did but I sold my mother's old wedding ring that I kept in my pocket so many years. The Italians are a humane people. They took the money and let me go but they told me not to peddle more.'

'So what do you do now?'

'I peddle. What should I do, beg? – I peddle. But last spring I got sick and gave my little money away to the doctors. I still have a bad cough.' He coughed fruitily. 'Now I have no capital to buy stock with. Listen, professor, maybe we can go in partnership together? Lend me twenty thousand lire and I will buy ladies' nylon stockings. After I sell them I will return you your money.'

'I have no funds to invest, Susskind.'

'You will get it back, with interest.'

'I honestly am sorry for you,' Fidelman said, 'but why don't you at least do something practical? Why don't you go to the Joint Distribution Committee, for instance, and ask them to assist you? That's their business.'

'I already told you why. They wish me to go back, I wish to stay here.'

'I still think going back would be the best thing for you.'

'No,' cried Susskind angrily.

'If that's your decision, freely made, then why pick on me? Am I responsible for you then, Susskind?'

'Who else?' Susskind loudly replied.

'Lower your voice, please, people are sleeping around

here,' said Fidelman, beginning to perspire. 'Why should I be?'

'You know what responsibility means?'

'I think so.'

'Then you are responsible. Because you are a man. Because you are a Jew, aren't you?'

'Yes, goddamn it, but I'm not the only one in the whole wide world. Without prejudice, I refuse the obligation. I am a single individual and can't take on everybody's personal burden. I have the weight of my own to contend with.'

He reached for his billfold and plucked out another dollar.

'This makes five. It's more than I can afford but take it and after this please leave me alone. I have made my contribution.'

Susskind stood there, oddly motionless, an impassioned statue, and for a moment Fidelman wondered if he would stay all night, but at last the refugee thrust forth a stiff arm, took the fifth dollar and departed.

Early the next morning Fidelman moved out of the hotel into another, less convenient for him, but far away from Shimon Susskind and his endless demands.

This was Tuesday. On Wednesday, after a busy morning in the library, Fidelman entered a near-by trattoria and ordered a plate of spaghetti with tomato sauce. He was reading his *Messaggero*, anticipating the coming of the food, for he was unusually hungry, when he sensed a presence at the table. He looked up, expecting the waiter, but beheld instead Susskind standing there, alas, unchanged.

Is there no escape from him? thought Fidelman, severely vexed. Is this why I came to Rome?

'Shalom, professor,' Susskind said, keeping his eyes off the table. 'I was passing and saw you sitting here alone, so I came in to say shalom.'

'Susskind,' Fidelman said in anger, 'have you been following me again?'

'How could I follow you?' asked the astonished Susskind. 'Do I know where you live now?'

Though Fidelman blushed a little, he told himself he owed nobody an explanation. So he had found out he had moved – good.

'My feet are tired. Can I sit five minutes?'

'Sit.'

Susskind drew out a chair. The spaghetti arrived steaming hot. Fidelman sprinkled it with cheese and wound his fork into several tender strands. One of the strings of spaghetti seemed to stretch for miles, so he stopped at a certain point and swallowed the forkful. Having foolishly neglected to cut the long string he was left sucking it, seemingly endlessly. This embarrassed him.

Susskind watched with rapt attention.

Fidelman at last reached the end of the long spaghetto, patted his mouth with a large napkin, and paused in his eating.

'Would you care for a plateful?'

Susskind, eyes hungry, hesitated. 'Thanks,' he said.

'Thanks yes or thanks no?'

'Thanks no.' The eyes looked away.

Fidelman resumed eating, carefully winding his fork; he had had not much practice with this sort of thing and was soon involved in the same dilemma with the spaghetti. Seeing Susskind still watching him, he soon became tense.

'We are not Italians, professor,' the refugee said. 'Cut it in small pieces with your knife. Then you will swallow it easier.'

'I'll handle it as I please,' Fidelman responded testily. 'This is my business. You attend to yours.'

'My business,' Susskind sighed, 'don't exist. This morning I had to let a wonderful chance get away from me. I had a chance to buy ladies' stockings at three hundred lire if I had money to buy half a gross. I could easily sell them for five hundred a pair. We would have made a nice profit.'

'The news doesn't interest me.'

'So if not ladies' stockings, I can also get sweaters, scarves, men's socks, also cheap leather goods, ceramics – whatever would interest you.'

'What interests me is what you did with the money I gave you for a sweater.'

'It's getting cold, professor,' Susskind said worriedly. 'Soon comes the November rains, and in winter the tramontana. I thought I ought to save your money to buy a couple of kilos of chestnuts and a bag of charcoal for my burner. If you sit all day on a busy street corner you can sometimes make a thousand lire. Italians like hot chestnuts. But if I do this I will need some warm clothes, maybe a suit.'

'A suit,' Fidelman remarked sarcastically, 'why not an overcoat?'

'I have a coat, poor that it is, but now I need a suit. How can anybody come in company without a suit?'

Fidelman's hand trembled as he laid down his fork. 'To my mind you are irresponsible and I won't be saddled with you. I have the right to choose my own problems and the right to my privacy.'

'Don't get excited, professor, it's bad for your digestion. Eat in peace.' Susskind got up and left the trattoria.

Fidelman hadn't the appetite to finish his spaghetti. He paid the bill, waited ten minutes, then departed, glancing around from time to time to see if he were being followed. He headed down the sloping street to a small piazza where he saw a couple of cabs. Not that he could afford one, but he wanted to make sure Susskind didn't tail him back to his new hotel. He would warn the clerk at the desk never to allow anybody of the refugee's name or description even to make inquiries about him.

Susskind, however, stepped out from behind a plashing fountain at the centre of the little piazza. Modestly addressing the speechless Fidelman, he said, 'I don't wish to take only, professor. If I had something to give you, I would gladly give it to you.'

'Thanks,' snapped Fidelman, 'just give me some peace of mind.'

'That you have to find yourself,' Susskind answered.

In the taxi Fidelman decided to leave for Florence the next day, rather than at the end of the week, and once and for all be done with the pest.

That night, after returning to his room from an unpleasurable walk in the Trastevere – he had a headache from too much wine at supper – Fidelman found his door ajar and at once recalled that he had forgotten to lock it, although he had as usual left the key with the desk clerk. He was at first frightened, but when he tried the armadio in which he kept his clothes and suitcase, it was shut tight. Hastily unlocking it, he was relieved to see his blue gabardine suit – a one-button jacket affair, the trousers a little frayed at the turn-ups but all in good shape and usable for years to come – hanging amid some shirts the maid had pressed for him; and when he examined the contents of the suitcase he found nothing missing, including, thank God, his passport and traveller's cheques. Gazing around the room, Fidelman saw all in place. Satisfied, he picked up a book and read ten pages before he thought of his brief-case. He jumped to his feet and began to search everywhere, remembering distinctly that it had been on the night table as he had lain on the bed that afternoon, re-reading his chapter. He searched under the bed and behind the night table, then again throughout the room, even on top of and behind the armadio. Fidelman hopelessly opened every drawer, no matter how small, but found neither the brief-case, nor, what was far worse, the chapter in it.

With a groan he sank down on the bed, insulting himself for not having made a copy of the manuscript, for he had more than once warned himself that something like this might happen to it. But he hadn't because there were some revisions he had contemplated making, and he had planned to retype the entire chapter before beginning the next. He thought now of complaining to the owner of the hotel, who lived on the floor below, but it was already past midnight and he realized nothing could be done until morning. Who could have taken it? The maid or hall porter? It seemed unlikely they would risk their jobs to steal a piece of leather goods that would bring them only a few thousand lire in a pawn shop. Possibly a sneak thief? He would ask tomorrow if other persons on the floor were missing something. He somehow doubted it. If a thief, he would then and there have ditched the chapter and stuffed the brief-case with Fidelman's oxblood shoes, left by the bed, and the fifteen-dollar R. H. Macy sweater that lay in full view on the desk. But if not the maid or porter or a sneak thief, then who? Though Fidelman had not the slightest shred of evidence to support his suspicions he could think of only one person – Susskind. This thought stung him. But if Susskind, why? Out of pique, perhaps, that he had not been given the suit he had coveted, nor was able to pry it out of the armadio?

Try as he would, Fidelman could think of no one else and no other reason. Somehow the peddler had followed him home (he had suspected their meeting at the fountain) and had got into his room while he was out to supper.

Fidelman's sleep that night was wretched. He dreamed of pursuing the refugee in the Jewish catacombs under the ancient Appian Way, threatening him a blow on the presumptuous head with a seven-flamed candelabrum he clutched in his hand; while Susskind, clever ghost, who knew the ins and outs of all the crypts and alleys, eluded him at every turn. Then Fidelman's candles all blew out, leaving him sightless and alone in the cemeterial dark; but when the student arose in the morning and wearily drew up the noisy blinds, the yellow Italian, somewhat shrunken, sun winked him cheerfully in both bleary eyes.

Fidelman postponed going to Florence. He reported his loss to the Questura, and though the police were polite and eager to help, they could do nothing for him. On the form on which the inspector noted the complaint, he listed the brief-case as worth ten thousand lire, and for 'valore del manoscritto' he drew a line. Fidelman, after giving the matter a good deal of thought, did not report Susskind, first, because he had absolutely no proof, for the desk clerk swore he had seen no stranger around in knickerbockers; second, because he was afraid of the consequences for the refugee if he were written down 'suspected' thief as well as 'unlicensed peddler' and inveterate refugee. He tried instead to rewrite the chapter, which he felt sure he knew by heart, but when he sat down at the desk there were important thoughts, whole paragraphs, even pages that went blank in the mind. He considered sending to America for his notes for the chapter but they were in a barrel in his sister's

27

attic in Levittown, among many notes for other projects. The thought of Bessie, a mother of five, poking around in his things, and the work entailed in sorting the cards, then getting them packaged and mailed to him across the ocean, wearied Fidelman unspeakably; he was certain she would send the wrong ones. He laid down his pen and went into the street, seeking Susskind. He searched for him in neighbourhoods where he had seen him before, and though Fidelman spent hours looking, literally days, Susskind never appeared; or if he perhaps did, the sight of Fidelman caused him to vanish. And when the student inquired about him at the Israeli consulate, the clerk, a new man on the job, said he had no record of such a person or his lost passport; on the other hand, the refugee was known at the JDC, but by name and address only, an impossibility, Fidelman thought. They gave him a number to go to but the place had long since been torn down to make way for an apartment house.

Time went without work, without accomplishment. To put an end to this appalling waste Fidelman tried to force himself back into his routine research and picture viewing. He moved out of the hotel, which he now could not stand for the harm it had done him (leaving a telephone number and urging to be called if the slightest clue turned up), and he took a room in a small pensione near the Stazione and here had breakfast and supper rather than go out. He was much concerned with expenditures and carefully recorded them in a notebook he had acquired for the purpose. Nights, instead of wandering in the city, feasting himself on its beauty and mystery, he kept his eyes glued to paper, sitting steadfastly at his desk in an attempt to re-create his initial chapter, because he was lost without a beginning. He had tried writing the second chapter from notes in his possession but it had come to nothing. Always Fidelman needed something solid behind him before he could advance, some worth-while accomplishment upon which to build another. He worked late but his mood, or inspiration, or whatever it was, had deserted him, leaving him with growing anxiety, almost disorientation; of not knowing – it seemed to him for the first time in months – what he must do next, a feeling that was torture. Therefore he again took up his search for the refugee. He thought now that once he had settled it, knew that the man had or hadn't stolen his chapter – whether he recovered it or not seemed at the moment immaterial – just the knowing of it would ease his mind and again he would feel like working, the crucial element.

Daily he combed the crowded streets, searching for Susskind wherever people peddled. On successive Sunday mornings he took the long ride to the Porta Portese market and hunted for hours among the piles of second-hand goods and junk lining the back streets, hoping his brief-case would magically appear, though it never did. He visited the open market at Piazza Fontanella Borghese, and observed the ambulant vendors at Piazza Dante. He looked among fruit and vegetable stalls set up in the streets, whenever he chanced upon them, and dawdled on busy street corners after dark, among beggars and fly-by-night peddlers. After the first cold snap at the end of October, when the chestnut sellers appeared throughout the city, huddled over pails of glowing coals, he sought in their faces the missing Susskind. Where in all of modern and ancient Rome was he? The man lived in the open air – he had to appear somewhere. Sometimes when riding in a bus or tram, Fidelman thought he had glimpsed somebody in a crowd, dressed in the refugee's clothes, and he invariably got off to run after whoever it was – once a man standing in front of the Banco di Santo Spirito, gone when Fidelman breathlessly arrived; and another time he overtook a person in knickerbockers but this one wore a monocle. Sir Ian Susskind?

In November it drearily rained. Fidelman wore a blue beret with his trench coat and a pair of black Italian shoes, smaller, despite their pointed toes, than his burly oxbloods which overheated his feet and whose colour he detested. But instead of visiting museums he frequented movie houses, sitting in the cheapest seats and regretting the cost. He was, at odd hours in certain streets, several times solicited by prostitutes, some heartbreakingly pretty, one a slender, unhappy-looking girl with bags under her eyes whom he desired mightily, but Fidelman feared for his health. He had got to know the face of Rome and spoke Italian fairly fluently but his heart was burdened, and in his blood raged a murderous hatred of the bandy-legged refugee – although there were times when he thought he might be wrong – so Fidelman more than once cursed him to perdition.

One Friday night, as the first star glowed over the Tiber, Fidelman, walking aimlessly along the left river bank, came upon a synagogue and wandered in among a crowd of Sephardim with Italianate faces. One by one they paused before a sink in an antechamber to dip their hands under a flowing tap, then in the house of worship touched with loose fingers their brows, mouths, and breasts as they bowed to the Ark, Fidelman doing likewise. Where in the world am I? Three rabbis rose from a bench and the service began, a long prayer, sometimes chanted, sometimes accompanied by invisible organ music, but no Susskind anywhere. Fidelman sat at a desk-like pew in the last row where he could inspect the congregants yet keep an eye on the door. The synagogue was unheated and the cold rose like an exudation from the marble floor. The student's freezing nose burned like a lit candle. He got up to go but the beadle, a stout man in a high hat and short caftan, wearing a long thick silver chain around his neck, fixed the student with his powerful left eye.

'From New York?' he inquired, slowly approaching.

Half the congregation turned to see who.

'State, not city,' answered Fidelman, nursing an active embarrassment for the attention he was attracting. Taking advantage of a pause, he whispered, 'Do you happen to know a man named Susskind? He wears knickerbockers.'

'A relative?' The beadle gazed at him sadly.

'Not exactly.'

'My own son – killed in the Ardeatine Caves.' Tears stood forth in his eyes.

'Ah, for that I'm sorry.'

But the beadle had exhausted the subject. He wiped his wet lids with pudgy fingers and the curious Sephardim turned back to their prayer books.

'Which Susskind?' the beadle wanted to know.

'Shimon.'

He scratched his ear. 'Look in the ghetto.'

'I looked.'

'Look again.'

The beadle walked slowly away and Fidelman sneaked out.

The ghetto lay behind the synagogue for several crooked well-packed blocks, encompassing aristocratic palazzi ruined by age and unbearable numbers, their discoloured façades strung with lines of withered wet wash, the fountains in the piazzas, dirt-laden, dry. And dark stone tenements, built partly on centuries-old ghetto walls, inclined towards one another across narrow, cobblestoned streets. In and among the impoverished houses were the wholesale establishments of wealthy Jews, dark holes ending in jewelled interiors, silks and silver of all colours. In the mazed streets wandered the present-day poor, Fidelman among them, oppressed by history although, he joked to himself, it added years to his life.

A white moon shone upon the ghetto, lighting it like dark day. Once he thought he saw a ghost he knew by sight, and hastily followed him through a thick stone passage to a blank wall where shone in white letters under a tiny electric bulb: VIETATO URINARE. Here was a smell but no Susskind.

For thirty lire the student bought a dwarfed blackened banana from a street vendor (not S) on a bicycle and stopped to eat. A crowd of ragazzi gathered to watch.

'Anybody here know Susskind, a refugee wearing knickerbockers?' Fidelman announced, stooping to point with the banana where the trousers went beneath the knees. He also made his legs a trifle bowed but nobody noticed.

There was no response until he had finished his fruit, then a thin-faced boy with brown liquescent eyes out of Murillo, piped: 'He sometimes works in the Campo Verano, the Jewish section.'

There too? thought Fidelman. 'Works in the cemetery?' he inquired. 'With a shovel?'

'He prays for the dead,' the boy answered, 'for a small fee.'

Fidelman bought him a quick banana and the others dispersed.

In the cemetery, deserted on the Sabbath – he should have come Sunday – Fidelman went among the graves, reading legends on tombstones, many topped with small brass candelabra, whilst withered yellow chrysanthemums lay on the stone tablets of other graves, dropped stealthily, he imagined, on All Souls' Day – a festival in another part of the cemetery – by renegade sons and daughters unable to bear the sight of their dead bereft of flowers whilst the crypts of the goyim were lit and in bloom. Many were burial places, he read on the stained stones, of those who, for one reason or another, had died in the late large war. Among them was an empty place, it said on a marble slab lying on the ground, for 'My beloved father/ Betrayed by the damned Fascists/ Murdered at Auschwitz by the barbarous Nazis/ *O Crimine Orribile*'.

— But no Susskind.

Three months had gone by since Fidelman's arrival in Rome. Should he, he many times asked himself, leave the city and this foolish search? Why not off to Florence, and there, amid the art splendours of the world, be inspired to resume his work? But the loss of his first chapter was like a spell cast over him. There were times he scorned it as a man-made thing, like all such, replaceable; other times he feared it wasn't the chapter per se, but that his volatile curiosity had become somehow entangled with Susskind's personality – Had he repaid generosity by stealing a man's life work? Was he so distorted? To satisfy himself, to know man, Fidelman had to know, though at what a cost in precious time and effort. Sometimes he smiled wryly at all this; ridiculous, the chapter grieved him for itself only – the precious thing he had created then lost – especially when he got to thinking of the long diligent labour, how painstakingly he had built each idea, how cleverly mastered problems of order, form, how impressive the finished product, Giotto reborn! It broke the heart. What else, if after months he was here, still seeking?

And Fidelman was unchangingly convinced that Susskind had taken it, or why would he still be hiding? He sighed much and gained weight. Mulling over his frustrated career, on the backs of envelopes containing unanswered letters from his sister Bessie he aimlessly sketched little angels flying. Once, studying his minuscule drawings, it occurred to him that he might some day return to painting but the thought was more painful than Fidelman could bear.

One bright morning in mid-December, after a good night's sleep, his first in weeks, he vowed he would have another look at the Navicella and then be off to Florence. Shortly before noon he visited the porch of St Peter's, trying, from his remembrance of Giotto's sketch, to see the mosaic as it had been before its many restorations. He hazarded a note or two in shaky handwriting, then left the church and was walking down the sweeping flight of stairs, when he beheld at the bottom – his heart misgave him, was he still seeing pictures, a sneaky apostle added to the overloaded boatful? – ecco, Susskind! The refugee, in beret and long green G.I. raincoat, from under whose skirts showed his black-stockinged rooster's ankles – indicating knickerbockers going on above though hidden – was selling black and white rosaries to all who would buy. He held several strands of beads in one hand, while in the palm of the other a few gilded medallions glinted in the winter sun. Despite his outer clothing, Susskind looked, it must be said, unchanged, not a pound more of meat or muscle, the face though aged, ageless. Gazing at him, the student ground his teeth in remembrance. He was tempted quickly to hide, and unobserved, observe the thief; but his impatience, after the long unhappy search, was too much for him. With controlled trepidation he approached Susskind on his left as the refugee was busily engaged on the right, urging a sale of beads upon a woman drenched in black.

'Beads, rosaries, say your prayers with holy beads.'

'Greetings, Susskind,' Fidelman said, coming shakily down the stairs, dissembling the Unified Man, all peace and contentment. 'One looks for you everywhere and finds you here. Wie gehts?'

Susskind, though his eyes flickered, showed no surprise to speak of. For a moment his expression seemed to say he had no idea who was this, had forgotten Fidelman's existence, but then at last remembered – somebody long ago from another country, whom you smiled on, then forgot.

'Still here?' he perhaps ironically joked.

'Still.' Fidelman was embarrassed at his voice slipping. 'Rome holds you?'

'Rome,' faltered the student, '— the air.' He breathed deep and exhaled with emotion.

Noticing the refugee was not truly attentive, his eyes roving upon potential customers, Fidelman, girding himself, remarked, 'By the way, Susskind, you didn't happen to notice – did you? – the brief-case I was carrying with me around the time we met in September?'

'Brief-case – what kind?' This he said absently, his eyes on the church doors.

'Pigskin. I had in it' – here Fidelman's voice could be heard cracking – 'a chapter of a critical work on Giotto I was writing. You know, I'm sure, the Trecento painter?'

'Who doesn't know Giotto?'

'Do you happen to recall whether you saw, if, that is —' He stopped, at a loss for words other than accusatory.

'Excuse me – business.' Susskind broke away and bounced

35

up the steps two at a time. A man he approached shied away. He had beads, didn't need others.

Fidelman had followed the refugee. 'Reward,' he muttered up close to his ear. 'Fifteen thousand for the chapter, and who has it can keep the brand-new brief-case. That's his business, no questions asked. Fair enough?'

Susskind spied a lady tourist, including camera and guide book. 'Beads – holy beads.' He held up both handsful, but she was just a Lutheran passing through.

'Slow today,' Susskind complained as they walked down the stairs, 'but maybe it's the items. Everybody has the same. If I had some big ceramics of the Holy Mother, they go like hot cakes – a good investment for somebody with a little cash.'

'Use the reward for that,' Fidelman cagily whispered, 'buy Holy Mothers.'

If he heard, Susskind gave no sign. At the sight of a family of nine emerging from the main portal above, the refugee, calling addio over his shoulder, fairly flew up the steps. But Fidelman uttered no response. I'll get the rat yet. He went off to hide behind a high fountain in the square. But the flying spume raised by the wind wet him, so he retreated behind a massive column and peeked out at short intervals to keep the peddler in sight.

At two o'clock, when St Peter's closed to visitors, Susskind dumped his goods into his raincoat pockets and locked up shop. Fidelman followed him all the way home, indeed the ghetto, although along a street he had not consciously been on before, which led into an alley where the refugee pulled open a left-handed door, and without transition, was 'home'. Fidelman, sneaking up close, caught a dim glimpse of an overgrown closet containing bed and table. He found no address on wall or door, nor, to his surprise,

36

any door lock. This for a moment depressed him. It meant Susskind had nothing worth stealing. Of his own, that is. The student promised himself to return tomorrow, when the occupant was elsewhere.

Return he did, in the morning, while the entrepreneur was out selling religious articles, glanced around once and was quickly inside. He shivered – a pitch-black freezing cave. Fidelman scratched up a thick match and confirmed bed and table, also a rickety chair, but no heat or light except a drippy candle stub in a saucer on the table. He lit the yellow candle and searched all over the place. In the table drawer a few eating implements plus safety razor, though where he shaved was a mystery, probably a public toilet. On a shelf above the thin-blanketed bed stood half a flask of red wine, part of a package of spaghetti, and a hard panino. Also an unexpected little fish bowl with a bony goldfish swimming around in Arctic seas. The fish, reflecting the candle flame, gulped repeatedly, threshing its frigid tail as Fidelman watched. He loves pets, thought the student. Under the bed he found a chamber pot, but nowhere a brief-case with a fine critical chapter in it. The place was not more than an ice-box someone probably had lent the refugee to come in out of the rain. Alas, Fidelman sighed. Back in the pensione, it took a hot water bottle two hours to thaw him out; but from the visit he never fully recovered.

In this latest dream of Fidelman's he was spending the day in a cemetery all crowded with tombstones, when up out of an empty grave rose this long-nosed brown shade, Virgilio Susskind, beckoning.

Fidelman hurried over.

'Have you read Tolstoy?'

37

'Sparingly.'

'Why is art?' asked the shade, drifting off.

Fidelman, willy-nilly, followed, and the ghost, as it vanished, led him up steps going through the ghetto and into a marble synagogue.

The student, left alone, because he could not resist the impulse, lay down upon the stone floor, his shoulders keeping strangely warm as he stared at the sunlit vault above. The fresco therein revealed this saint in fading blue, the sky flowing from his head, handing an old knight in a thin red robe his gold cloak. Near by stood a humble horse and two stone hills.

Giotto. San Francesco dona le vesti al cavaliere povero.

Fidelman awoke running. He stuffed his blue gabardine into a paper bag, caught a bus, and knocked early on Susskind's heavy portal.

'Avanti.' The refugee, already garbed in beret and raincoat (probably his pyjamas), was standing at the table, lighting the candle with a flaming sheet of paper. To Fidelman the paper looked the underside of a typewritten page. Despite himself the student recalled in letters of fire his entire chapter.

'Here, Susskind,' he said in a trembling voice, offering the bundle, 'I bring you my suit. Wear it in good health.'

The refugee glanced at it without expression. 'What do you wish for it?'

'Nothing at all.' Fidelman laid the bag on the table, called good-bye and left.

He soon heard footsteps clattering after him across the cobblestones.

'Excuse me, I kept this under my mattress for you.' Susskind thrust at him the pigskin brief-case.

Fidelman savagely opened it, searching frantically in

each compartment, but the bag was empty. The refugee was already in flight. With a bellow the student started after him. 'You bastard, you burned my chapter!'

'Have mercy,' cried Susskind, 'I did you a favour.'

'I'll do you one and cut your throat.'

'The words were there but the spirit was missing.'

In a towering rage Fidelman forced a burst of speed, but the refugee, light as the wind in his marvellous knicker-bockers, green coat-tails flying, rapidly gained ground.

The ghetto Jews, framed in amazement in their medieval windows, stared at the wild pursuit. But in the middle of it, Fidelman, stout and short of breath, moved by all he had lately learned, had a triumphant insight.

'Susskind, come back,' he shouted, half sobbing. 'The suit is yours. All is forgiven.'

He came to a dead halt but the refugee ran on. When last seen he was still running.

2

Months after vainly seeking a studio on the Vie Margutta, del Babuino, della Croce, and elsewhere in that neighbourhood, Arthur Fidelman settled for part of a crowded, windowy, attic-like atelier on a cobblestone street in the Trastevere, strung high with sheets and underwear. He had, a week before, in 'personal notices' in the American language newspaper in Rome, read: 'Studio to share, cheap, many advantages, etc., A. Oliovino,' and after much serious anguish (the curt advertisement having recalled dreams he had dreamed were dead), many indecisions, enunciations and renunciations, Fidelman had, one very cold late-December morning, hurried to the address given, a worn four-storey building with a yellowish façade stained brown along the edges. On the top floor, in a thickly cluttered artist's studio smelling aromatically of turpentine and oil paints, the inspiring sight of an easel lit in unwavering light from the three large windows setting the former art student on fire once more to paint, he had dealt not with a pittore, as expected, but with a pittrice, Annamaria Oliovino.

The pittrice, a thin, almost gaunt, high-voiced restless type, with short black uncombed hair, violet mouth, distracted eyes and a tense neck, a woman with narrow buttocks and piercing breasts, was in her way attractive if not in truth beautiful. She had on a thick black woollen sweater, eroded black velveteen culottes, black socks, and leather sandals spotted with drops of paint. Fidelman and she eyed each other stealthily and he realized at once she was, as a woman, indifferent to him or his type, who or which made no difference. But after ten minutes, despite the turmoil she exuded even as she dispassionately answered his hesitant questions, Fidelman, ever a sucker for strange beauty and all sorts of experiences, felt himself involved with and falling for her. Not my deep dish, he warned himself, aware of all the dangers to him and his renewed desire to create art; yet he was already half in love with her. It can't be, he thought in desperation; but it could. It had happened to him before. In her presence he tightly shut both eyes and whole-heartedly wished against what might be. Really he trembled, and though he laboured to extricate his fate from hers, he was already a plucked bird, greased, and ready for frying. Fidelman loudly protested within – cried out severely against the weak self, called himself ferocious names but could do not much, a victim of his familiar response, a too passionate fondness for strangers. So Annamaria, who had advertised a twenty thousand lire monthly rental, in the end doubled the sum, and Fidelman paid through both nos-trils, cash for first and last months (should he attempt to fly by night) plus a deposit of ten thousand for possible damages. An hour later he moved in with his imitation leather suit-case. This happened in the dead of winter. Below the cold sunlit windows stood two frozen umbrella pines and be-yond, in the near distance, sparkled the icy Tiber.

The studio was well heated, Annamaria had insisted, but the cold leaked in through the wide windows. It was more a blast; the art student shivered but was kept warm by his hidden love for the pittrice. It took him most of a day to clear himself a space to work, about a third of the studio was as much as he could manage. He stacked her canvasses five deep against her portion of the walls, curious to examine them, but Annamaria watched his every move (he noticed several self-portraits) although she was at the same time painting a monumental natura morta of a loaf of bread with two garlic bulbs ('Pane ed Agli'). He moved stacks of *Oggi*, piles of postcards and yellowed letters, and a bundle of calendars going back to many years ago; also a Perugina candy box full of broken pieces of Etruscan pottery, one of small sea shells, and a third of medallions of various saints and of the Virgin, which she warned him to handle with care. He had uncovered a sagging cot by a dripping stone sink in his corner of the studio and there he slept. She furnished an old chafing dish and a broken table, and he bought a few household things he needed. Annamaria rented the art student an easel for a thousand lire a month. Her quarters were private, a room at the other end of the studio whose door she kept locked, handing him the key when he had to use the toilet. The wall was thin and the instrument noisy. He could hear the whistle and rush of her water, and though he tried to be quiet, because of the plumbing the bowl was always brimful and the pour of his stream embarrassed him. At night, if there was need, although he was tempted to use the sink, he fished out the yellowed, sedimented pot under his bed; once or twice, as he was using it in the thick of night, he had the impression she was awake and listening.

They painted in their overcoats, Annamaria wearing a black babushka, Fidelman a green wool hat pulled down over his frozen ears. She kept a pan of hot coals at her feet and every so often lifted a sandalled foot to toast it. The marble floor of the studio was sheer thick ice; Fidelman wore two pairs of tennis socks his sister Bessie had recently sent him from the States. Annamaria, a leftie, painted with a smeared leather glove on her hand, and theoretically his easel had been arranged so that he couldn't see what she was doing but he often sneaked looks at her work. The pittrice, to his surprise, painted with flicks of her fingers and wrists, peering at her performance with almost shut eyes. He noticed she alternated still lifes with huge lyric abstractions – massive whorls of red and gold exploding, these built on, entwined with, and ultimately concealing a small religious cross, her first two brush strokes on every canvas. Once when Fidelman gathered the nerve to ask her why the cross, she answered it was the symbol that gave the painting its meaning.

'What meaning?'

'The meaning I want it to have.'

He was eager to know more but she was impatient. 'Eh,' she shrugged, 'who can explain art.'

Though her response to his various attempts to become better acquainted were as a rule curt, and her voluntary attention to him, shorter still – she was able, apparently, to pretend he wasn't there – Fidelman's feeling for Annamaria grew, and he was as unhappy in love as he had ever been.

But he was patient, a persistent virtue, served her often in various capacities, for instance carrying down four flights of stairs her two bags of garbage shortly after supper – the portinaia was crippled and the portiere never around – sweeping the studio clean each morning, even running to retrieve a brush or paint tube when she happened to drop one – offering any service any time, you name it. She accepted these small favours without giving them notice.

One morning after reading a many-paged letter she had just got in the mail, Annamaria was sad, sullen, unable to work; she paced around restlessly, it troubled him. But after feverishly painting a widening purple spiral that continued off the canvas, she regained a measure of repose. This heightened her beauty, lent it somehow a youthful quality it didn't ordinarily have – he guessed her to be no older than twenty-seven or -eight; so Fidelman, inspired by the change in her, hoping it might foretoken better luck for him, approached Annamaria, removed his hat and suggested since she went out infrequently why not lunch for a change at the trattoria at the corner, Guido's, where workmen assembled and the veal and white wine were delicious? She, to his surprise, after darting an uneasy glance out of the window at the tops of the motionless umbrella pines, abruptly assented. They ate well and conversed like human beings, although she mostly limited herself to answering his modest questions. She informed Fidelman she had come from Naples to Rome two years ago, although it seemed much longer, and he told her he was from the United States. Being so physically close to her, able to inhale the odour of her body – like salted flowers – and intimately eating together, excited Fidelman, and he sat very still, not to rock the boat and spill a drop of what was so precious to him. Annamaria ate hungrily, her eyes usually lowered. Once she looked at him with a shade of a smile and he felt beatitude; the art student contemplated many such meals though he could ill afford them, every cent he spent, saved and sent by Bessie.

After zuppa inglese and a peeled apple she patted her lips with a napkin, and still in good humour, suggested they take the bus to the Piazza del Popolo and visit some painter friends of hers.

'I'll introduce you to Alberto Moravia.'

'With pleasure,' Fidelman said.

But when they stepped into the street and were walking

to the bus stop near the river a cold wind blew up and Annamaria turned pale.

'Something wrong?' Fidelman inquired.

'The East Wind.' She spoke testily.

'What wind?'

'The Evil Eye,' she said with irritation. 'Malocchio.'

He had heard something of the sort. They returned
quickly to the studio, their heads lowered against the noisy
wind, the pittrice from time to time furtively crossing herself. A black-habited old nun passed them at the trattoria
corner, from whom Annamaria turned in torment, mutter-
ing 'Jettatura! Porca miseria!' When they were upstairs
in the studio she insisted Fidelman touch his testicles three
times to undo or dispel who knew what witchcraft, and he
modestly obliged. Her request had inflamed him, although
he cautioned himself to remember, it was in purpose and
essence theological.

Later she received a visitor, a man who came to see her
on Monday and Friday afternoons after his work in a
government bureau. Her visitors, always men, whispered
with her a minute, then left restlessly; most of them, except-
ing also Giancarlo Balducci, a cross-eyed illustrator –
Fidelman never saw again. But the one who came oftenest
stayed longest, a solemn grey-haired gent, Augusto Otto-
galli, with watery blue eyes and missing side teeth, old enough
to be her father for sure. He wore a slanted black fedora and
a shabby grey overcoat too large for him, greeted Fidelman vacantly and made him inordinately jealous. When
Augusto arrived in the afternoon the pittrice usually dropped anything she was doing and they retired to her room, at
once noisily locked and bolted. The art student wandered
alone in the studio for dreadful hours. When Augusto ultimately emerged, looking dishevelled, and if successful,

defeated, Fidelman turned his back on him and the old man hastily let himself out of the door. After his visits, and only his, Annamaria did not appear in the studio for the rest of the day. Once when Fidelman knocked on her door to invite her out to supper, she said to use the pot because she had a headache and was sound asleep. On another occasion when Augusto was locked long in her room with her, after a tormenting two hours Fidelman tiptoed over and put his jealous ear to the door. All he could hear was the buzz and sigh of their whispering. Peeking through the keyhole he saw them both in their overcoats, sitting on her bed, Augusto clasping her hands, whispering passionately, his nose empurpled with emotion, Annamaria's white face averted. When the art student checked an hour later, they were still at it, the old man imploring, the pittrice weeping. The next time, Augusto came with a priest, a portly, heavy-breathing man with a doubtful face. But as soon as they appeared in the studio Annamaria, enraged to fury, despite the impassioned entreatments of Augusto, began to throw at them anything of hers or Fidelman's she could lay hands on.

'Bloodsuckers!' she shouted, 'scorpions! parasites!' until they had hastily retreated. Yet when Augusto, worn and harried, returned alone, without complaint she retired to her room with him.

Fidelman's work, despite the effort and despair he gave it, was going poorly. Every time he looked at unpainted canvas he saw harlequins, whores, tragic kings, fragmented musicians, the sick and the dread. Still, tradition was tradition and what if he wanted to make more? Since he had always loved art history he considered embarking on a 'Mother and Child', but was afraid her image would come out too much

46

Bessie – after all, a dozen years between them. Or maybe a moving 'Pietà', the dead son's body held like a broken wave in mama's frail arms? A curse on art history – he fought the fully prefigured picture though some of his former best paintings had jumped in every detail to the mind. Yet if so where's true engagement? Sometimes I'd like to forget every picture I've seen, Fidelman thought. Almost in panic he sketched in charcoal a coat-tailed 'Figure of a Jew Fleeing' and quickly hid it away. After that, ideas, prefigured or not, were scarce. 'Astonish me,' he muttered, wondering whether to return to surrealism. He also considered a series of 'Relations to Places and Space', hard-edge constructions in squares and circles, the pleasures of tri-dimensional geometry of linear abstraction, only he had little heart for it. The furthest abstraction, Fidelman thought, is the blank canvas. A moment later he said to himself, if painting shows who you are why should not painting? I mean I oughtn't to worry about that.

After the incident with the priest Annamaria was despondent for a week, stayed in her room sometimes bitterly crying, Fidelman often standing helplessly by her door. However, her unhappy mood was prelude to a burst of creativity by the pittrice. Works by the dozens leaped from her brush and stylus. She went on with her lyric abstractions based on the theme of a hidden cross and spent hours with a long black candle, burning holes in heavy white paper ('Buchi Spontanei'). Having mixed coffee grounds, sparkling bits of crushed mirror and ground sea shells, she blew the dust on mucilaged paper ('Velo nella Nebbia'). She composed collages of rags and toilet paper. After a dozen linear studies ('Linee Discendenti'), she experimented with gold leaf sprayed with umber, the whole while wet drawn in long undulations with a fine comb. She framed this in a black frame and hung it on end like a diamond ('Luce di Candela'). Annamaria worked intently, her brow furrowed, violet mouth tightly pursed, eyes lit, nostrils palpitating in creative excitement; and when she had temporarily run out of new ideas she did a mythological bull in red clay ('La Donna Toro'), afterwards returning to natura morta with bunches of bananas; then self-portraits.

The pittrice occasionally took time out to see what Fidelman was up to, although not much, and then editing his efforts. She changed lines and altered figures, or swabbed paint over whole compositions that didn't appeal to her. There was not much that did, but Fidelman was grateful for any attention she gave his work, and even kept at it to incite her criticism. He could feel his heartbeat in his teeth whenever she stood close to him modifying his work, he deeply breathing her intimate smell of sweating flowers. She wore perfume only when Augusto came and it disappointed Fidelman that the old man should evoke the use of bottled fragrance; yet he was cheered that her natural odour which he, so to say, got for free, was so much more exciting than the stuff she doused herself with for her decrepit Romeo. He had noticed she had a bit of soft belly but he loved the pliant roundness and often day-dreamed of it. Thinking it might please her, for he pleased her rarely (he reveried how it would be once she understood the true depth of his love for her), the art student experimented with some of the things Annamaria had done – spontaneous holes, for instance, several studies of 'Lines Ascending', and two lyrical abstract expressionistic pieces based on, interwoven with, and ultimately concealing a Star of David, although for these attempts he soon discovered he had earned, instead of her good will, an increased measure of scorn.

However, Annamaria continued to eat lunch with him

at Guido's, and more often than not, supper, although she said practically nothing during meals and afterwards let her eye roam over the faces of the men at the other tables. But there were times after they had eaten when she would agree to go for a short walk with Fidelman, if there was no serious wind; and once in a while they entered a movie in the Trastevere, for she hated to cross any of the bridges of the Tiber, and then only in a bus, sitting stiffly, staring ahead. As they were once riding Fidelman seized the opportunity to hold her tense fist in his, but as soon as they were safely across the river she tore it out of his grasp. He was by now giving her presents – tubes of paints, the best brushes, a few yards of Belgian linen, which she accepted without comment; she also borrowed small sums from him, nothing startling – a hundred lire today, five hundred tomorrow. And she announced one morning that he would thereafter, since he used so much of both, have to pay additional for water and electricity – he already paid extra for the heatless heat. Fidelman, though always worried about money, assented. He would give his last lira to lie on her soft belly, but she offered niente, not so much as a caress; until one day he was permitted to look on as she sketched herself nude in his presence. Since it was bitter cold the pittrice did this in two stages. First she removed her sweater and brassière, and viewing herself in a long faded mirror, quickly sketched the upper half of her body before it turned blue. He was dizzily enamoured of her form and flesh. Hastily fastening the brassière and pulling on her sweater, Annamaria stepped out of her sandals and peeled off her culottes, and white panties torn at the crotch, then drew the rest of herself down to her toes. The art student begged permission to sketch along with her but the pittrice denied it, so he had, as best one can, to commit to memory her lovely treasures – the

49

hard, piercing breasts, narrow shapely buttocks, vine-hidden labia, the font and sweet beginning of time. After she had drawn herself and dressed, and when Augusto appeared and they had retired behind her bolted door, Fidelman sat motionless on his high stool before the glittering blue-skied windows, slowly turning to ice to faint strains of Bach.

The art student increased his services to Annamaria; her increase was scorn, or so it seemed. This severely bruised his spirit. What have I done to deserve such treatment? That I pay my plenty of rent on time? That I buy her all sorts of presents, not to mention two full meals a day? That I live in flaming hot and freezing cold? That I passionately adore each sweet-and-sour bit of her? He figured it bored her to see so much of him. For a week Fidelman disappeared during the day, sat in cold libraries or moved around in frosty museums. He tried painting after midnight and into the early morning hours but the pittrice found out and unscrewed the bulbs before she went to bed. 'Don't waste my electricity, this isn't America.' He screwed in a dim blue bulb and worked silently from 1 a.m. to five. At dawn he discovered he had painted a blue picture. Fidelman wandered in the streets of the city. At night he slept in the studio and could hear her sleeping in her room. She slept restlessly, dreamed badly, and often moaned. He dreamed he had three eyes and was missing an ear, or nose.

For two weeks he spoke to no one but a dumpy four-and-a-half foot female on the third floor, and to her usually to say no. Fidelman, having often heard the music of Bach drifting up from below, had tried to picture the lady piano player, imagining a quiet blonde with a slender body, a woman of grace and beauty. It had turned out to be Clelia Montemaggio, a middle-aged old maid music teacher, who sat at the old upright piano, her apartment door open to let out the cooking smells, particularly fried fish on Friday. Once when coming up from taking down the garbage, Fidelman had paused to listen to part of a partita at her door and she had lassoed him in for an espresso and pastry. He ate and listened to Bach, her plump bottom moving spryly on the bench as she played not badly.

'Lo spirito,' she called to him raptly over her shoulder, 'l'architettura!'

Fidelman nodded. Thereafter whenever she spied him in the hall she attempted to entice him with cream-filled pastries and J.S.B., whom she played apparently exclusively.

'Come een,' she called in English, 'I weel play for you. We weel talk. There is no use for too much solitude.' But the art student, burdened by his, spurned hers.

Unable to work, he wandered in the streets in a desolate mood, his spirit dusty in a city of fountains and leaky water taps. Water, water everywhere, spouting, flowing, dripping, whispering secrets, love love love, but not for him. If Rome's so sexy, where's mine? Fidelman's Romeless Rome. It belonged least to those who yearned most for it. With slow steps he climbed the Pincio, if possible to raise his spirits gazing down at the rooftops of the city, spires, cupolas, towers, monuments, compounded history and past time. It was in sight, possessable, all but its elusive spirit; after so long he was still straniero. He was then struck by a thought: if you could paint this sight, give it its quality in yours, the spirit belonged to you. History become aesthetic! Fidelman's scalp thickened. A wild rush of things he might paint swept sweetly through him: saints in good and bad health, whole or maimed, in gold and red; nude grey rabbis at Auschwitz, black or white Negroes – what not when *any* colour dripped from your brush? And if these, so also

51

ANNAMARIA ES PULCHRA. He all but cheered. What more intimate possession of a woman! He would paint her, whether she permitted or not, posed or not – she was his to paint, he could with eyes shut. Maybe something will come, after all, of my love for her. His spirits elevated, Fidelman ran most of the way home.

It took him eight days, a labour of love. He tried her as nude and although able to imagine every inch of her, could not commit it to canvas. Then he suffered until it occurred to him to paint her as 'Virgin with Child'. The idea astonished and elated him. Fidelman went feverishly to work and caught an immediate likeness in paint. Annamaria, saintly beautiful, held in her arms the infant resembling his little nephew Georgie. The pittrice, aware, of course, of his continuous activity, cast curious glances his way, but Fidelman, painting in the corner by the stone sink, kept the easel turned away from her. She pretended unconcern. Done for the day he covered the painting and carefully guarded it. The art student was painting Annamaria in a passion of tenderness for the infant at her breast, her face responsive to its innocence. When, on the ninth day, in trepidation Fidelman revealed his work, the pittrice's eyes clouded and her underlip curled. He was about to grab the canvas and smash it up all over the place when her expression fell apart. The art student postponed all movement but trembling. She seemed at first appalled, a darkness descended on her, she was undone. She wailed wordlessly, then sobbed, 'You have seen my soul.' They embraced tempestuously, her breasts stabbing him, Annamaria bawling on his shoulder. Fidelman kissed her wet face and salted lips, she murmuring as he fooled with the hook of her brassière under her sweater, 'Aspetta, aspetta, caro, viene Augusto.' He was mad with expectation and suspense.

Augusto, who usually arrived punctually at four, did not appear that Friday afternoon. Uneasy as the hour approached, Annamaria seemed relieved as the streets grew dark. She had worked badly after viewing Fidelman's painting, sighed frequently, gazed at him with sweet-sad smiles. At six she gave in to his urging and they retired to her room, his unframed 'Virgin with Child' already hanging above her bed, replacing a gaunt self-portrait. He was curiously disappointed in the picture – surfacy thin – and made a mental note to borrow it back in the morning to work on it more. But the conception, at least, deserved the reward. Annamaria cooked supper. She cut his meat for him and fed him forkfuls. She peeled Fidelman's orange and stirred sugar in his coffee. Afterwards, at his nod, she locked and bolted the studio and bedroom doors and they undressed and slipped under her blankets. How good to be for a change on this side of the locked door, Fidelman thought, relaxing marvellously. Annamaria, however, seemed tensely alert to the noises of the old building, including a parrot screeching, some shouting kids running up the stairs, a soprano singing 'Ritorna, vincitor!' But she calmed down and hotly embraced Fidelman. In the middle of a passionate kiss the doorbell rang.

Annamaria stiffened in his arms. 'Diavolo! Augusto!'

'He'll go away,' Fidelman advised. 'Both doors locked.'

But she was at once out of bed, pulling on her culottes. 'Get dressed,' she said.

He hopped up and hastily got into his trousers.

Annamaria unlocked and unbolted the inner door and then the outer. It was the postman waiting to collect ten lire for an overweight letter from Naples.

After she had read the long letter and wiped away a tear they undressed and got back into bed.

'Who is he to you?' Fidelman asked.

'Who?'

'Augusto.'

'An old friend. Like a father. We went through much
together.'

'Were you lovers?'

'Look, if you want me take me. If you like to ask questions
go back to school.'

He determined to mind his business.

'Warm me,' Annamaria said, 'I'm freezing.'

Fidelman stroked her slowly. After ten minutes she said,
'"Gioco di mano, gioco di villano." Use your imagination.'

He used his imagination and she responded with excitement. 'Dolce tesoro,' she whispered, flicking the tip of her
tongue into his ear, then with little bites biting his ear lobe.

The doorbell rang loudly.

'For Christ's sake, don't answer,' Fidelman groaned. He
tried to hold her down but she was already up, hunting her
robe.

'Put on your trousers,' she hissed.

He had thoughts of waiting for her in bed but it ended
with his dressing fully. She sent him to the door. It was the
crippled portinaia, the art student having neglected to take
down the garbage.

Annamaria furiously got the two bags and handed them to
her.

In bed she was so cold her teeth chattered.

Tense with desire Fidelman warmed her.

'Angelo mio,' she murmured. 'Amore, possess me.'

He was about to when she kicked her legs together and
hastily rose. 'The cursed door again!'

Fidelman gnashed his teeth. 'I heard nothing.'

In her torn yellow silk robe she hurried to the front

door, opened and shut it, quickly locked and bolted it, did the same in her room and slid into bed.

'You were right, it was nobody.'

She embraced him, her hairy armpits perfumed. He responded with postponed passion.

'Enough of antipasto,' Annamaria said. She reached for his member.

Overwrought, Fidelman, though fighting himself not to, spent himself in her hand. Although he mightily willed resurrection, his wilted flower bit the dust.

She furiously shoved him out of bed, into the studio, flinging his clothes after him.

'Pig, beast, onanist!'

At least she lets me love her. Daily Fidelman shopped, cooked, and cleaned for her. Every morning he took her shopping sack off the hook, went down to the street market and returned with the bag stuffed full of greens, pasta, eggs, meat, cheese, wine, bread. Annamaria insisted on three hearty meals a day although she had once told him she no longer enjoyed eating. Twice he had seen her throw up her supper. What she enjoyed he didn't know except it wasn't Fidelman. After he had served her at her table he was allowed to eat alone in the studio. At two every afternoon she took her siesta and though it was forbidden to make noise, he was allowed to wash the dishes, dust and clean her room, swab the toilet bowl. She called 'Fatso' and in he trotted to get her anything she had run out of – drawing pencils, sanitary belt, safety pins. After she awoke from her nap, rain or shine, please or no please, he was now compelled to leave the studio so she could work in peace and quiet. He wandered, in the tramontana, from one cold two-bit movie to another. At seven he was back to prepare her

supper, and twice a week Augusto's, who sported a new
black hat and spiffy overcoat, and pitied the art student
with both wet blue eyes but wouldn't look at him. After
supper, another load of dishes, the garbage downstairs,
and when Fidelman returned, with or without Augusto
Annamaria was already closeted behind her bolted door.
He checked through the keyhole on Mondays and Fridays
but she and the old gent were always fully clothed. Fidelman
had more than once complained to her that his punishment
exceeded his crime, but the pittrice said he was a type she
would never have any use for. In fact he did not exist for
her. Not existing how could he paint, although he told himself he must? He couldn't. He aimlessly froze wherever he
went, a mean cold that seared his lungs though under his
overcoat he wore a new thick sweater Bessie had knitted for
him, and two woollen scarves around his neck. Since the
night Annamaria had kicked him out of bed he had not
been warm; yet he often dreamed of ultimate victory. Once
when he was on his lonely way out of the house – a night she
was giving a party for some painter friends, Fidelman, a
drooping butt in the corner of his mouth, carrying the
garbage bags, met Clelia Montemaggio coming up the stairs.

'You look like a frozen board,' she said. 'Come in and
enjoy the warmth and a little Bach.'

Unable to unfreeze enough to say no, he continued down
with the garbage.

'Every man gets the woman he deserves,' she called after
him.

'Who got,' Fidelman muttered. 'Who gets.'

He considered jumping into the Tiber but it was full of
ice that winter.

One night at the end of February, Annamaria, to Fidelman's astonishment – it deeply affected him – said he

might go with her to a party at Giancarlo Balducci's studio on the Via dell' Oca; she needed somebody to accompany her in the bus across the bridge and Augusto was flat on his back with the Asian 'flu. The party was lively – painters, sculptors, some writers, two diplomats, a prince and a visiting Hindu sociologist, their ladies and three hotsy-totsy, scantily dressed, unattached girls. One of them, a shapely beauty with orange hair, green eyes, and warm ways became interested in Fidelman, except that he was dazed by Annamaria, seeing her in a dress for the first time, a ravishing rich ruby-coloured affair. The cross-eyed host had provided simply a huge cut-glass bowl of spiced mulled wine, and the guests dipped ceramic glasses into it and guzzled away. Everyone but the art student seemed to be enjoying himself. One or two of the men disappeared into other rooms with female friends or acquaintances and Annamaria, in a gay mood, did a fast shimmy to rhythmic handclapping. She was drinking steadily and when she wanted her glass filled, politely called him 'Arturo'. He began to have mild thoughts of possibly possessing her.

The party bloomed, at least forty, and turned wildish. Practical jokes were played. Fidelman discovered his left shoe had been smeared with mustard. Balducci's black cat mewed at a fat lady's behind, a slice of sausage pinned to her dress. Before midnight there were two fist fights, Fidelman enjoying both but not getting involved though once he was socked on the neck by a sculptor who had aimed at a painter. The girl with the orange hair, still interested in the art student, invited him to join her in Balducci's bedroom but he continued to be devoted to Annamaria, his eyes tied to her every move. He was jealous of the illustrator, who whenever near her nipped her bottom.

One of the sculptors, Orazio Pinello, a slender man

57

with a darkish face, heavy black brows, and bleached blond hair, approached Fidelman. 'Haven't we met before, caro?'

'Maybe,' the art student said, perspiring lightly. 'I'm Arthur Fidelman, an American painter.'

'You don't say? Action painter?'

'Always active.'

'I refer of course to Abstract Expressionism.'

'Of course. Well, sort of. On and off.'

'Haven't I seen some of your work around? Galleria Schneider? Some symmetric hard-edge biomorphic forms? Not bad as I remember.'

Fidelman thanked him, in full blush.

'Who are you here with?' Orazio Pinello asked.

'Annamaria Oliovino.'

'Her?' said the sculptor. 'But she's a fake.'

'Is she?' Fidelman said with a sigh.

'Have you looked at her work?'

'With one eye. Her art is bad but I find her irresistible.'

'Peccato.' The sculptor shrugged and drifted away.

A minute later there was another fist fight, during which the green-eyed orange head conked Fidelman with a Chinese vase. He went out cold and when he came to, Annamaria and Balducci were undressing him in the illustrator's bedroom. Fidelman experienced an almost overwhelming pleasure, then Balducci explained that the art student had been chosen to pose in the nude for drawings both he and the pittrice would do of him. He explained there had been a discussion as to which of them did male nudes best and they had decided to settle it in a short contest. Two easels had been wheeled to the centre of the studio; a half hour was allotted to the contestants, and the guests would judge who had done the better job. Though he at first objected because it was a cold night, Fidelman nevertheless felt warmish from wine so he agreed to pose; besides he was proud of his muscles and maybe if she sketched him nude it might arouse her interest in a tussle later. And if he wasn't painting he was at least being painted.

So the pittrice and Giancarlo Balducci, in paint-smeared smocks, worked for thirty minutes by the clock, the whole party silently looking on, with the exception of the orange-haired tart, who sat in the corner eating a prosciutto sandwich. Annamaria, her brow furrowed, lips pursed, drew intensely with crayon; Balducci worked calmly in coloured chalk. The guests were absorbed, although after ten minutes the Hindu went home. A journalist locked himself in the painter's bedroom with orange head and would not admit his wife who pounded furiously on the door. Fidelman, standing barefoot on a rubber bathmat, was eager to see what Annamaria was accomplishing but had to be patient. When the half hour was up he was permitted to look. Balducci had drawn a flock of green and black abstract testiculate circles. Fidelman shuddered. But Annamaria's drawing was representational, not Fidelman although of course inspired by him: A gigantic funereal phallus that resembled a broken-backed snake. The blond sculptor inspected it with half-closed eyes, then yawned and left. By now the party was over, the guests departed, lights out except for a few dripping white candles. Balducci was collecting his ceramic glasses and emptying ash-trays, and Annamaria had thrown up. The art student afterwards heard her begging the illustrator to sleep with her but Balducci complained of fatigue.

'I will if he won't,' Fidelman offered.

Annamaria, enraged, spat on her picture of his unhappy phallus.

'Don't dare come near me,' she cried. 'Malocchio! Jettatura!'

The next morning he awoke sneezing, a nasty cold. How can I go on? Annamaria, showing no signs of pity or remorse, continued shrilly to berate him. 'You've brought me nothing but bad luck since you came here. I'm letting you stay because you pay well but I warn you to stay out of my sight.'

'But how —' he asked hoarsely.

'That doesn't concern me.'

'— how will I paint?'

'Who cares? Paint at night.'

'Without light —'

'Paint in the dark. I'll give you a can of black paint.'

'How can you be so cruel to a man who loves —'

'I'll scream,' she said.

He left in anguish. Later while she was at her siesta he came back, got some of his things and tried to paint in the hall. No dice. Fidelman wandered in the rain. He sat for hours on the Spanish Steps. Then he returned to the house and went slowly up the stairs. The door was locked. 'Annamaria,' he hoarsely called. Nobody answered. In the street he stood at the river wall, watching the dome of St Peter's in the distance. Maybe a potion, Fidelman thought, or an amulet? He doubted either would work. How do you go about hanging yourself? In the late afternoon he went back to the house – would say he was sick, needed rest, possibly a doctor. He felt feverish. She could hardly refuse.

But she did, although explaining she felt bad herself. He held on to the banister as he went downstairs. Clelia Montemaggio's door was open. Fidelman paused, then continued down but she had seen him. 'Come een, come een.'

He went reluctantly in. She fed him camomile tea and panettone. He ate in a wolfish hurry as she seated herself at the piano.

'No Bach, please, my head aches from various troubles.'

'Where's your dignity?' she asked.

'Try Chopin, that's lighter.'

'Respect yourself, please.'

Fidelman removed his hat as she began to play a Bach prelude, her bottom rhythmic on the bench. Though his cold oppressed him and he could hardly breathe, tonight the spirit, the architecture, moved him. He felt his face to see if he were crying but only his nose was wet. On the top of the piano Clelia had placed a bowl of white carnations in full bloom. Each white petal seemed a white flower. If I could paint those gorgeous flowers, Fidelman thought. If I could paints omething. By Jesus, if I could paint myself, that'd show them! Astonished by the thought he ran out of the house.

The art student hastened to a costume shop and settled on a cassock and fuzzy black soup-bowl biretta, envisaging another Rembrandt: 'Portrait of the Artist as Priest'. He hurried with his bulky package back to the house. Annamaria was handing the garbage to the portinaia as Fidelman thrust his way into the studio. He quickly changed into the priest's vestments. The pittrice came in wildly to tell him where he got off, but when she saw Fidelman already painting himself as priest, with a moan she rushed into her room. He worked with smoking intensity and in no time created an amazing likeness. Annamaria, after stealthily re-entering the studio, with heaving bosom and agitated eyes closely followed his progress. At last, with a cry, she threw herself at his feet.

'Forgive me, Father, for I have sinned —'

Dripping brush in hand, he stared down at her. 'Please, I —'

'Oh, Father, if you knew what I've done. I've been a whore —'

After a moment's thought Fidelman said, 'If so I absolve you.'

'Not without penance. First listen to the rest. I've had no luck with men, they're all bastards. Or else I jinx them. If you want the truth I'm an Evil Eye myself. Anybody who loves me is cursed.'

He listened in fascination.

'Augusto is really my uncle. After many others he became my lover. At least he's gentle. My father found out and swore he'd kill us both. That's when I left Naples. I was pregnant and scared to death. A sin can go too far. Augusto told me to have the baby and leave it at an orphanage, but the night it was born I was confused and threw it into the Tiber. I was afraid it was an idiot.'

She was sobbing. He drew back.

'Wait,' she wept. 'The next time in bed Augusto was impotent. Since then he's been imploring me to confess so he can get back his powers. But every time I step into the confessional my tongue turns to bone. The priest can't tear a word out of me. That's how it's been all my life, don't ask me why because I don't know.'

She grabbed his knees. 'Help me, Father, for Christ's sake.'

Fidelman, after a short tormented time, said in a quavering voice, 'I forgive you, my child.'

'The penance,' she wailed, 'first the penance.'

After reflecting, he replied, 'Say one hundred times each, Our Father and Hail Mary.'

'More,' Annamaria wept. 'More, more. Much more.'

Gripping his knees so hard they shook she burrowed her head into his black-buttoned lap. He felt the surprised beginnings of an erection.

'In that case,' Fidelman said, shuddering a little, 'better undress.'

'Only,' Annamaria said, 'if you keep your vestments on.'

'Not the cassock, too clumsy.'

'At least the biretta.'

He agreed to that.

Annamaria undressed in a swoop. Her body was extraordinarily lovely, the flesh glowing. In her bed they tightly embraced. She clasped his buttocks, he cupped hers. Pumping slowly he nailed her to her cross.

3

Fidelman listlessly doodles all over a sheet of yellow paper. Odd indecipherable designs, ink-spotted blotched words, esoteric ideographs, tormented figures in a steaming sulphurous lake, a stylish nude rising newborn out of cold water. Not bad at all though more mannequin than Knidean Aphrodite. Scarpio, sharp-nosed on the former art student's gaunt left, looking up from his cards, inspects her with his good eye.

'Not bad, who is she? One of the girls here?'

'Nobody I really know.'

'You must be hard up.'

'I always am.'

'Quiet,' rumbles Angelo, the padrone, on Fidelman's far right, his two-chinned face moulded in lard. He flips the top card.

Scarpio turns up a deuce, making eight and a half and out. He curses his Sainted Mother, Angelo wheezing. Fidelman shows four and his last hundred lire. He picks a cautious ace and sighs. Angelo, with seven showing, chooses this passionate moment to relieve himself.

'Wait for me,' he orders. 'Watch the pot, Scarpio.'

'Who's that hanging?' Scarpio points to a long-coated figure loosely dangling from a gallows rope amid Fidelman's other doodles.

Who but Susskind, surely. A dim figure out of the past.

'Just a friend. Nobody you know.'

'It'd better not be.'

Scarpio picks up the yellow paper for a closer squint.

'But whose head?' he asks with interest. A long-nosed severed head bounces down the steps of the guillotine platform.

A man's head or his sex, Fidelman wonders. In either case a terrible wound.

'Looks a little like mine. At least the long jaw.'

Scarpio points to a street scene. In front of American Express here's this starving white Negro pursued by a hooting mob of cowboys on horses.

Embarrassed by the recent past Fidelman blushes.

Long past midnight. They sit motionless in Angelo's stuffy office, a small lit bulb glowing darkly over a square wooden table on which lie a pack of puffy cards, Fidelman's naked hundred lire note, and a green bottle of Munich beer that the padrone of the Hotel du Ville, Milano, swills from between hands and games. Scarpio, his major-domo and secretary-lover, sips an espresso. Fidelman only watches, being without privileges. Each night they play sette e mezzo, jeenrummy, or baccarat and Fidelman loses the day's earnings, the few meagre tips he has garnered from the whores for little services rendered. Angelo says nothing and takes all.

Scarpio, snickering, understands the street scene. Fidelman, adrift penniless in the stony grey Milanese streets, had picked his first pocket. An American tourist staring into a store window. The Texan, feeling the tug, and missing his wallet, had bellowed murder. A carabiniere looked wildly at Fidelman, who broke into a run, another well-dressed carabiniere on a horse clattering after him down the street, waving his sword over his head. Angelo, cleaning his fingernails with his penknife in front of his hotel, saw Fidelman coming pell-mell and ducked him around a corner, through a cellar door, into the Hotel du Ville, a joint for prostitutes who split fees with the padrone for the use of a room.

Angelo registered the former art student, gave him a tiny dark room, and pointing a gun, relieved him of his passport and the contents of the Texan's wallet. He warned him that if he ratted to anybody, he would report him to the Questura where his brother presided, as a dangerous alien thief. The former art student, desperate to escape, needed money to travel, so he sneaked into Angelo's room one morning and from the strapped suitcase under the bed, extracted fistfuls of lire, stuffing all his pockets. Scarpio, happening in, caught him at it and held a dagger to Fidelman's ribs – who fruitlessly pleaded they could both make a living from the suitcase – until the padrone appeared.

'A hunchback is straight only in his grave.'

Angelo slapped Fidelman's face first with one fat hand, then with the other, till it turned red and the tears flowed freely. He chained him to the bed in his room for a week. When Fidelman promised to behave he was released and appointed mastro delle latrine, having to clean thirty toilets daily with a stiff brush, for room and board. He also assisted Teresa, the asthmatic, hairy-legged chambermaid, and ran errands for the whores. The former art student hoped to escape but the portiere or his assistant was at the door twenty-four hours a day. And thanks to the card games and his impassioned gambling, Fidelman was without sufficient funds to go anywhere, if there was anywhere to go. And without passport, so he stayed put.

Scarpio secretly feels Fidelman's thigh.

'Let go or I'll tell the padrone.'

66

Angelo returns and flips up a card. Queen. Seven and a half on the button. He pockets Fidelman's last hundred lire.

'Go to bed,' says Angelo, 'it's a long day tomorrow.'

Fidelman climbs up to his room on the fifth floor and stares out of the window into the dark street to see how far down is death. Too far, so he undresses for bed. He looks every night and sometimes during the day. Teresa, screaming, had once held on to his two legs as Fidelman dangled half out of the window until one of the girls' naked customers, a barrel-chested man, rushed into the room and dragged him back in.

Sometimes Fidelman weeps in his sleep.

He awakes, cringing. Angelo and Scarpio are in his room but nobody hits him.

'Search anywhere,' Fidelman offers. 'You won't find a thing except maybe half a stale pastry.'

'Shut up,' says Angelo. 'We want to make a proposition.'

Fidelman slowly sits up. Scarpio produces the yellow sheet of scribbled fantasies. 'We notice you draw.' He points a dirty fingernail at the nude figure.

'After a fashion. I doodle and see what happens.'

'Could you copy a painting?'

'What sort of painting?'

'Just a nude. Tiziano's 'Venus of Urbino'. The one after Giorgione.'

'Oh that one?' Fidelman thinks. 'I doubt that I could.'

'Any fool can.'

'Shut up, Scarpio.' Angelo sits his bulk at the foot of Fidelman's narrow bed. Scarpio, with his good eye, moodily inspects the cheerless view from the window.

'On Isola Bella in Lago Maggiore, about an hour from

here,' Angelo says, 'there's a small castello full of lousy paintings, except for one which is a genuine Tiziano, authenticated by three art experts, including a brother-in-law of mine. It's worth half a million dollars but the owner is richer than Olivetti and won't sell though an American museum has offered a fortune.'

'Very interesting.'

'Exactly. Anyway it's insured for at least $400,000. Of course if anyone stole it it would be impossible to sell.'

'Then why bother?'

'Bother what?'

'Whatever it is,' Fidelman says lamely.

'You'll learn more by listening. Suppose it was stolen and held for ransom?'

'Ransom?'

'Ransom,' Scorpio says from the window.

'At least $300,000,' says Angelo, 'a bargain for the insurance company. They'd save a hundred thousand on the deal.'

He outlines a plan. They had photographed the Titian on both sides from all angles and distances and had collected from various art books the best colour plates. They also had the exact measurements of the canvas and every figure on it. If Fidelman could make a decent copy they would duplicate the frame and on a dark night sneak the reproduction into the castello gallery and exit with the original. The guards were stupid and the advantage of the plan – instead of slitting the canvas out of its frame – was that nobody would recognize the substitution for days, possibly longer. In the meantime they would row the picture across the lake and truck it out of the country; one had a better chance in France. Once the picture was securely hidden, Angelo back at the hotel, Scorpio would get in touch with the insurance company. Recognizing the brilliance of the execution, they would kick in at once with the ransom money.

'If you make a good copy you'll get yours,' said Angelo.

'Mine? What would that be?' Fidelman asks.

'Your passport,' Angelo answers cagily. 'Plus two hundred American dollars and a quick good-bye.'

'Five hundred dollars,' says Fidelman.

'Scarpio,' the padrone says patiently, 'show him what you have in your trousers.'

Scarpio unbuttons his jacket and draws a mean-looking dagger from a sheath under his belt.

'Three-fifty,' Fidelman says. 'I'll need plane fare.'

'Three-fifty,' nods Angelo. 'Payable when you deliver the finished reproduction.'

'And you pay for all supplies?'

'All expenses within reason. But if you try any monkey tricks – snitch or double cross, you'll wake up with your head missing, or something worse.'

'Tell me,' Fidelman says after a minute of contemplation, 'what if I turn down the proposition? I mean in a friendly way?'

Angelo rises sternly from the creaking bed. 'Then you'll stay here for the rest of your life. When you leave you leave in a coffin, very cheap wood.'

'I see.'

'Then it's settled,' says Angelo.

'Take the morning off,' says Scarpio.

'Thanks.'

The padrone glares. 'First finish the toilet bowls.'

Am I worthy? Can I do it? Do I dare? He has these and other doubts, feels melancholy, and wastes time.

Angelo one morning calls him into his office. 'Have a Munich beer.'

'No, thanks.'

'Cordial?'

'Nothing now.'

'What's the matter with you? You look as if you buried your mother.'

Fidelman sets down his mop and pail and says nothing.

'Why don't you put those things away and get started?' the padrone asks. 'I've had the portiere move six trunks and some broken furniture out of the storeroom where you have two big windows. Scarpio wheeled in an easel and he's bought you brushes, colours and anything else you need.'

'It's west light, not very even.'

Angelo shrugs. 'It's the best I can do. This is our season and I can't spare any other rooms. If you'd rather work at night we can set up some lamps. It's a waste of electricity but I'll make that concession to your temperament if you work fast and produce the goods.'

'What's more I don't know the first thing about forging paintings. All I might do is just about copy the picture.'

'That's all we ask. Leave the technical business to us. First do a decent drawing. When you're ready to paint I'll get you a piece of sixteenth-century Belgian linen that's been scraped clean of a former picture. You prime it with white lead and when it's dry you sketch. Once you finish the nude, Scarpio and I will bake it, put in the cracks, and age them with soot. We'll even stipple in fly spots before we varnish and glue. We'll do what's necessary. There are books on this subject and Scarpio reads like a demon. It isn't as complicated as you think.'

'What about the truth of the colours?'

'I'll mix them for you. I've made a life study of Tiziano's work.'

Fidelman's eyes are still unhappy.

'What's eating you now?'

'It's stealing another painter's ideas and work.'

The padrone wheezes. 'Tiziano will forgive you. Didn't he steal the figure of the Urbino from Giorgione? Didn't Rubens steal the Andrian nude from Tiziano? Art steals and so does everybody. You stole a wallet and tried to steal my lire. What's the difference? It's the way of the world. We're only human.'

'It's a sort of desecration.'

'Everybody desecrates. We live off the dead and they live off us. Take for instance religion.'

'I doubt I can do it without seeing the original,' Fidelman says. 'The colour plates you gave me aren't true.'

'Neither is the original any more. You don't think Rembrandt painted in those sfumato browns? As for painting the Venus, you'll have to do the job here. If you copied it in the castello gallery one of those cretin guards might remember your face and next thing you know you'd be in trouble. So would we, which we wouldn't want, naturally.'

'I still ought to see it.'

The padrone reluctantly consents to a one-day excursion to Isola Bella, assigning Scarpio to closely accompany the copyist.

On the vaporetto to the island, Scarpio, wearing dark glasses and a light straw hat, turns to Fidelman.

'In all confidence what do you think of Angelo?'

'He's all right I guess. Why?'

'Do you think he's handsome?'

'Maybe he was once.'

'You have many fine insights,' Scarpio says. He points in the distance where the long blue lake disappears amid towering Alps. 'Locarno, sixty kilometers.'

'Is that so?' With Switzerland so close freedom swells in Fidelman's heart but he does nothing about it. Scarpio clings to him as to a virgin cousin, and sixty kilometers is a long swim with a knife in your back.

'That's the castello over there,' the major-domo says. 'It looks like a joint.'

The castello is pink on a high terraced hill amid tall trees in formal gardens. It is full of tourists and bad paintings. But in the last gallery, 'infinite riches in a little room', hangs the 'Venus of Urbino' alone.

What a miracle, Fidelman thinks.

The golden brown-haired Venus, a woman of the real world, lies on her couch in serene beauty, her hand lightly touching her intimate mystery, the other holding red flowers, her nude body her truest accomplishment.

'I'd have painted somebody in bed with her,' Scarpio says.

'Shut up,' says Fidelman.

Scarpio, hurt, leaves the gallery.

Fidelman, alone with Venus, worships the painting. What magnificent tones, what extraordinary flesh that turns the body into spirit.

While Scarpio is out talking to the guard, the copyist hastily sketches the Venus, and with a Leica Angelo has given him for the purpose, takes several new colour shots.

Afterwards he approaches the picture and kisses the lady's hands, thighs, and breasts, but as he murmurs, 'I love you,' a guard strikes him hard on the head with both fists.

That night as they are returning on the rapido to Milano,

Scarpio falls asleep, snoring. He awakens in a hurry, tugging at his dagger, but Fidelman hasn't moved.

The copyist throws himself into his work with passion. He has swallowed lightning and hopes it will strike whatever he touches. Yet he has nagging doubts he can do the job right and fears he will never escape alive from the Hotel du Ville. He tries at once to paint the Titian directly on canvas but hurriedly scrapes it clean when he sees what a garish mess he has made. The Venus is insanely disproportionate and the maids in the background foreshortened into dwarfs. He then takes Angelo's advice and makes several drawings on paper to master the composition before committing it again to canvas.

Angelo and Scarpio come up every night and shake their heads over the drawings.

'Not even close,' says the padrone.

'Far from it,' says Scarpio.

'I'm trying,' Fidelman says, anguished.

'Try harder,' Angelo answers grimly.

Fidelman has a sudden insight. 'What happened to the last guy who tried?'

'He's still floating,' Scarpio says.

'I'll need some practice,' the copyist coughs. 'My vision seems tight and the arm tires easily. I'd better go back to exercises to loosen up.'

'What kind of exercises?' Scarpio inquires.

'Nothing physical, just some warm-up nudes to get me going.'

'Don't overdo it,' Angelo says. 'You've got about a month, not much more. There's an advantage to making the exchange of pictures during the tourist season.'

'Only a month?'

The padrone nods.

'Maybe you'd better trace it,' Scarpio suggests.

'No.'

'I'll tell you what,' says Angelo. 'I could find you an old reclining nude you can paint over. You might get the form of this one by altering the form of another.'

'It's not honest, I mean to myself.'

Everyone titters.

'Well, it's your headache,' says Angelo.

Fidelman, unwilling to ask what happens if he fails, after they leave, feverishly draws faster.

Things go badly for the copyist. Working all day and often into the very early morning hours, he tries everything he can think of. Since he always distorts the figure of Venus, though he carries it perfect in his mind, he goes back to a study of Greek statuary with ruler and compass to compute the mathematical proportions of the ideal nude. Scarpio accompanies him to one or two museums. Fidelman also works with the Vetruvian square in the circle, experiments with Dürer's intersecting circles and triangles, and studies Leonardo's schematic heads and bodies. Nothing doing. He draws paper dolls, not women, certainly not Venus. He draws girls who will not grow up. He then tries sketching every nude he can lay eyes on in the art books Scarpio brings him from the library; from the Esquiline goddess to 'Les Demoiselles d'Avignon'. Fidelman copies not badly many figures from classical statuary and modern painting; but when he returns to his Venus, with something of a laugh she eludes him. What am I, bewitched, the copyist asks himself, and if so by whom? It's only a copy job so what's taking so long? He can't even guess, until he happens to see a naked whore cross the hall to enter a friend's room. Maybe the ideal is cold and I like it hot? Nature over art?

Inspiration – the live model? Fidelman knocks on the door and tries to persuade the girl to pose for him but she can't for economic reasons. Neither will any of the others – there are four girls in the room.

A red-head among them calls out to Fidelman, 'Shame on you, Arturo, are you too good to bring up pizzas and coffee any more?'

'I'm busy on a job for Angelo. Painting a picture, that is. A business proposition.'

Their laughter further depresses his spirits. No inspiration from whores. Maybe too many naked women around make it impossible to draw a nude. Still he'd better try a live model, having tried everything else and failed.

In desperation, on the verge of panic because time is going so fast, he thinks of Teresa, the chambermaid. She is a poor specimen of feminine beauty but the imagination can enhance anything. Fidelman asks her to pose for him, and Teresa, after a shy laugh, consents.

'I will if you promise not to tell anybody.'

Fidelman promises.

She undresses, a meagre, bony girl, breathing heavily, and he draws her with flat chest, distended belly, thin hips and hairy legs, unable to alter a single detail. Van Eyck would have loved her. When Teresa sees the drawing she weeps profusely.

'I thought you would make me beautiful.'

'I had that in mind.'

'Then why didn't you?'

'It's hard to say,' says Fidelman.

'I'm not in the least bit sexy,' Teresa weeps.

Considering her body with half-closed eyes, Fidelman tells her to go borrow a long slip.

'Get one from one of the girls and I'll draw you sexy.'

She returns in a frilly white slip and looks so attractive that instead of painting her, Fidelman, with a lump in his throat, gets her to lie down with him on a dusty mattress in the room. Clasping her slip-encased form, the copyist shuts both eyes and concentrates on his elusive Venus. He feels about to recapture a rapturous experience and is looking forward to it but at the last minute it turns into a limerick he didn't know he knew:

> "Whilst Titian was mixing rose madder,
> His model was crouched on a ladder;
> Her position to Titian suggested coition,
> So he stopped mixing madder and had'er."

Angelo, entering the storeroom just then, lets out a bellow. He fires Teresa on her naked knees pleading with him not to, and Fidelman has to go back to latrine duty the rest of the day.

'You might as well keep me doing this permanently,' Fidelman, disheartened, tells the padrone in his office afterwards. 'I'll never finish that cursed picture.'

'Why not? What's eating you? I've treated you like a son.'

'I'm blocked, that's what.'

'Get to work, you'll feel better.'

'I just can't paint.'

'For what reason?'

'I don't know.'

'Because you've had it too good here.' Angelo angrily strikes Fidelman across the face. When the copyist sobs, he boots him hard in the rear.

That night Fidelman goes on a hunger strike but the padrone, hearing of it, threatens forced-feeding.

After midnight Fidelman steals some clothes from a sleeping whore, dresses quickly, ties on a kerchief, makes up his eyes and lips, and walks out of the door past Scarpio sitting on a bar stool, enjoying the night breeze. Having gone a block, fearing he will be chased, Fidelman breaks into a high-heeled run but it's too late. Scarpio has recognized him in afterthought and yells for the portiere. Fidelman kicks off his slippers and runs furiously but the skirt impedes him. The major-domo and portiere catch up with him and drag him, kicking and struggling, back to the hotel. A carabiniere, hearing the commotion, appears on the scene, but seeing how Fidelman is dressed, will do nothing for him. In the cellar Angelo hits him with a short rubber hose until he collapses.

Fidelman lies in bed three days, refusing to eat or get up.

'What'll we do now?' Angelo, worried, whispers. 'How about a fortune teller? Either that or let's bury him.'

'Astrology is better,' Scarpio says. 'I'll check his planets. If that doesn't work we'll try psychology. He's a suggestible type.'

'Well, make it fast.'

Scarpio tries astrology but it doesn't work: a mix-up of Venus with Mars he can't explain; so the next morning he tries psychology. He comes into Fidelman's room with a thick book under his arm. The art copyist is still in bed, smoking a butt.

'Do you believe in psycho-analysis?'

'Sort of.'

'Maybe we'd better try that. I'm here to help you. Don't get up.'

Scarpio opens the book to its first chapter. 'The thing to do is associate freely.'

'What's the point of this?'

'It might loosen you up. Do you have any memories of

your mother? For instance, did you ever see her naked?'

'She died young,' Fidelman says, on the verge of tears. 'I was raised by my sister Bessie.'

'Go on, I'm listening,' says Scarpio.

'I can't. My mind goes blank.'

Scarpio turns to the next chapter, flips through several pages, then rises with a sigh.

'It might be a medical matter. Take a physic tonight.'

'I already have.'

The major-domo shrugs. 'Life is complicated. Anyway, keep track of your dreams. Write them down as soon as you have them.'

Fidelman puffs his butt.

That night he dreams of Bessie about to bathe. He is peeking at her through the bathroom keyhole as she prepares her bath. Open-mouthed he watches her remove her robe and step into the tub. Her hefty well-proportioned body then is young and full in the right places; and in the dream Fidelman, then fourteen, looks at her with longing that amounts to anguish. The older Fidelman, the dreamer, considers doing a 'La Baigneuse' right then and there, but when Bessie begins to soap herself with Ivory soap, the boy slips into her room, opens her poor purse, filches fifty cents for the movies, and goes on tiptoes down the stairs.

He is shutting the vestibule door with great relief when Arturo Fidelman awakes with a headache in Milano. As he scribbles down his dream he suddenly remembers what Angelo had said: 'Everybody steals. We're all human.'

A stupendous thought occurs to him: Suppose he personally steals the picture?

A marvellous idea all around. Fidelman heartily eats that morning's breakfast.

*　　*　　*　　*　　*

To steal the picture he had to paint one. Within another day the copyist successfully sketches Titian's painting and then begins to work in oils on an old piece of Flemish linen that Angelo had hastily supplied him with after seeing the successful drawing. Fidelman underpaints the canvas and after it is dry begins the figure of Venus as the conspirators look on sucking their breaths.

'Stay relaxed,' begs Angelo, sweating. 'Don't spoil it now. Remember you're painting the appearance of a picture. The original has already been done. Give us a decent copy and we'll do the rest with chemistry.'

'I'm worried about the brush strokes.'

'Nobody will notice them. Just keep in your mind that Tiziano painted resolutely with few strokes, his brush loaded with colour. In the end he would paint with his fingers. We don't ask for perfection, just a good copy.'

He rubs his fat hands nervously.

But Fidelman paints as though he were painting the original. He works alone late at night, when the conspirators are snoring, and he paints with what is left of his heart. He has caught the figure of the Venus but when it comes to her flesh, her thighs and breasts, he thinks he will never make it. As he paints he seems to remember every nude that has ever been done, Fidelman satyr, with Silenus beard and goatlegs, piping and peeking at backside, frontside, or both, at the 'Rokeby Venus', 'Bathsheba', 'Suzanna'. 'Venus Anadyomene', 'Olympia'; at picnickers in dress or undress, bathers ditto, Vanitas or Truth, Niobe or Leda, in chase or embrace, hausfrau or whore, amorous ladies modest or brazen, single or in crowds at the Turkish bath, in every conceivable shape or position, while he sports and disports until a trio of maenads pull his tail and he gallops after them through the dusky woods. He is at the same time choked by remembered lust for all the women he had ever desired, from Bessie to Annamaria Oliovino, and for their garters, underpants, slips or half-slips, brassières and stockings. Although thus tormented, Fidelman feels himself falling in love with the one he is painting, every inch of her, including the ring on her pinky, bracelet on arm, the flowers she touches with her fingers, and the bright green ear-ring that dangles from her eatable ear. He would have prayed her alive if he weren't certain she would fall in love, not with her famished creator, but surely the first Apollo Belvedere she lays eyes on. Is there, Fidelman asks himself, a world where love endures and is always satisfying? He answers in the negative. Still she is his as he paints, so he goes on, planning never to finish, to be happy in loving her, thus for ever happy.

But he finishes the picture on a Saturday night, Angelo's gun pressed to his head. Then the Venus is taken from him and Scarpio and Angelo bake, smoke, stipple and varnish, stretch and frame Fidelman's masterwork as the artist lies on his bed in his room in a state of collapse.

'The Venus of Urbino, c'est moi.'

'What about my three hundred and fifty?' Fidelman asks Angelo during a card game in the padrone's stuffy office several days later. After finishing the painting the copyist is again back on janitorial duty.

'You'll collect when we've got the Tiziano.'

'What about my passport?'

'Give it to him, Scarpio.'

Scarpio hands him the passport. Fidelman flips through the booklet and sees all the pages intact.

'If you skiddoo now,' Angelo warns him, 'you'll get spit.'

80

'Who's skiddooing?'

'So the plan is this: You and Scarpio will row out to the castello after midnight. The caretaker is an old man and half deaf. You hang our picture and breeze off with the other.'

'If you wish,' Fidelman suggests, 'I'll gladly do the job myself. Alone, that is.'

'Why alone?' Scarpio asks suspiciously.

'Don't be foolish,' Angelo says. 'With the frame it weighs half a ton. Now listen to directions and don't give any. One reason I detest Americans is they never know their place.'

Fidelman apologizes.

'I'll follow in the putt-putt and wait for you half-way between Isola Bella and Stresa in case we need a little extra speed at the last minute.'

'Do you expect trouble?'

'Not a bit. If there's any trouble it'll be your fault. In that case watch out.'

'Off with his head,' says Scarpio. He plays a deuce and takes the pot.

Fidelman laughs politely.

The next night, Scarpio rows a huge weatherbeaten boat, both oars muffled. It is a moonless night with touches of Alpine lightning in the distant sky. Fidelman sits on the stern, holding with both hands and balancing against his knees, the large framed painting, heavily wrapped in monk's cloth and cellophane and tied around with rope.

At the island the major-domo docks the boat and secures it. Fidelman, peering around in the dark, tries to memorize where they are. They carry the picture up two hundred steps, both puffing when they get to the formal gardens on top.

81

The castello is black except for a square of yellow light from the caretaker's turret window high above. As Scarpio snaps the lock of an embossed heavy wooden door with a strip of celluloid, the yellow window slowly opens and an old man peers down. They freeze against the wall until the window is drawn shut.

'Fast,' Scarpio hisses. 'If anyone sees us they'll wake the whole island.'

Pushing open the creaking door, they quickly carry the painting, growing heavier as they hurry, through an enormous room cluttered with cheap statuary, and by the light of the major-domo's flashlight, ascend a narrow flight of spiral stairs. They hasten in sneakers down a deep-shadowed tapestried hall into the picture gallery, Fidelman stopping in his tracks when he beholds the Venus, the true and magnificent image of his counterfeit creation.

'Let's get to work.' Scarpio quickly unknots the rope and they unwrap Fidelman's painting and lean it against the wall. They are taking down the Titian when footsteps sound unmistakably in the hall. Scarpio's flashlight goes out.

'Sh, it's the caretaker. If he comes in I'll have to conk him.'

'That'll kill Angelo's plan – deceit, not force.'

'I'll think of that when we're out of here.'

They press their backs to the wall, Fidelman's clammy, as the old man's steps draw nearer. The copyist has anguished visions of losing the picture and makes helterskelter plans somehow to reclaim it. Then the footsteps falter, come to a stop, and after a minute of intense hesitation, move in another direction. A door slams and the sound is gone.

It takes Fidelman several seconds to breathe. They wait in the dark without moving until Scarpio shines his light.

Both Venuses are resting against the same wall. The major-domo closely inspects each canvas with one eye shut, then signals the painting on the left. 'That's the one, let's wrap it up.'

Fidelman breaks into profuse sweat.

'Are you crazy? That's mine. Don't you know a work of art when you see it?' He points to the other picture.

'Art?' says Scarpio, removing his hat and turning pale. 'Are you sure?' He peers at the painting.

'Without a doubt.'

'Don't try to confuse me.' He taps the dagger under his coat.

'The lighter one is the Titian,' Fidelman says through a hoarse throat. 'You smoked mine a shade darker.'

'I could have sworn yours was the lighter.'

'No, Titian's. He used light varnishes. It's a historical fact.'

'Of course.' Scarpio mops his brow with a dirty handkerchief. 'The trouble is with my eyes. One is in bad shape and I over-use the other.'

'That's tough,' clucks Fidelman.

'Anyway, hurry up. Angelo's waiting on the lake. Remember, if there's any mistake he'll cut your throat first.'

They hang the darker painting on the wall, quickly wrap the lighter and hastily carry it through the long hall and down the stairs, Fidelman leading the way with Scarpio's light.

At the dock the major-domo nervously turns to Fidelman. 'Are you absolutely sure we have the right one?'

'I give you my word.'

'I accept it but under the circumstances I'd better have another look. Shine the light through your fingers.'

Scarpio kneels to undo the wrapping once more, and

Fidelman trembling, brings the flashlight down hard on his straw hat, the light shattering in his hand. The major-domo, pulling at his dagger, collapses.

Fidelman has trouble loading the painting into the row-boat but finally gets it in and settled, and quickly takes off. In ten minutes he had rowed out of sight of the dark castled island. Not long afterwards he thinks he hears Angelo's putt-putt behind him. His heart beats erratically but the padrone does not appear. He rows hard as the waves deepen.

Locarno, sixty kilometres.

A wavering flash of lightning pierces the broken sky, lighting the agitated lake all the way to the Alps, as a dreadful thought assails Fidelman: had he the right paint-ing? After a minute he pulls in his oars, listens once more for Angelo, and hearing nothing, steps to the stern of the rowboat, letting it drift as he frantically unwraps the Venus.

In the pitch black, on the lake's choppy waters, he sees she is indeed his, and by the light of numerous matches adores his handiwork.

4

F, ravaged Florentine, grieving, kicked apart a trial canvas,
copy of one he had been working on for years, his foot
through the poor mother's mouth, destroyed the son's in-
sipid puss, age about ten. It deserved death for not coming
to life. He stomped on them both, but not of course on the
photograph still tacked to the easel ledge, sent years ago by
sister Bessie, together with her last meagre cheque. 'I
found this old photo of you and Momma when you were a
little boy. Thought you might like to have it, she's been
dead these many years.' Inch by enraged inch he rent the
canvas, though cheap linen he could ill afford, and would
gladly have cremated the remains if there were a place to.
He swooped up the mess with both hands, grabbed some
smeared drawings, ran down four rickety flights and dumped
all in the bowels of a huge burlap rubbish bag in front of the
scabby mustard-walled house on Via S. Agostino. Fabio,
the embittered dropsical landlord, asleep on his feet, awoke
and begged for a few lire back rent but F ignored him.
Across the broad piazza, Santo Spirito, nobly proportioned,
stared him in the bushy moustached face, but he would not
look back. His impulse was to take the nearest bridge and
jump off into the Arno, flowing again in green full flood after
a dry summer; instead, he slowly ascended the stairs, pelted

by the landlord's fruity curses. Upstairs in his desolate studio he sat on his bed and wept. Then he lay with his head at the foot of the bed and wept.

The painter blew his nose at the open window and gazed, for a reflective hour at the Tuscan hills in September haze. Otherwise, sunlight on the terraced silver-trunked olive trees, and San Miniato, sparkling, framed in the distance by black cypresses. Make an interesting impressionist oil, green and gold mosaics and those black trees of death, but that's been done. Not to mention Van Gogh's tormented cypresses. That's my trouble, everything's been done or is otherwise out of style – cubism, surrealism, action painting. If I could only guess what's next. Below, a stunted umbrella pine with a headful of black and white chirping swallows grew in the landlord's narrow yard, over a dilapidated henhouse that smelled to heaven, except that up here the smell was sweetened by the odour of red roof tiles. A small dirty white rooster crowed shrilly, the shrimpy brown hens clucking as they ran in dusty circles around three lemon trees in tubs. F's studio was a small room with a curtained kitchen alcove – several shelves, a stove and sink – the old-fashioned walls painted with faded rustic dancers, nymphs and shepherds, and on the ceiling a large scalloped cornucopia full of cracked and faded fruit.

He looked until the last of morning was gone, then briskly combed his thick moustache, sat at the table and ate a hard anise biscuit as his eyes roamed over some quotations he had stencilled on the wall.

Constable: 'Painting is for me another word for feeling.'

Whistler: 'A masterpiece is finished from the beginning.'

Pollock: 'What is it that escapes me? The human? That humanity is greater than art?'

Nietzsche: 'Art is not an imitation of nature but its

86

metaphysical supplement, raised up beside it in order to overcome it.'

Picasso: 'People seize on painting in order to cover up their nakedness.'

Ah, if I had his genius.

Still, he felt better, picked up a fourteen-inch Madonna he had carved and sanded it busily. Then he painted green eyes, black hair, pink lips and a sky-blue cloak, and waited around smoking until the statuette had dried. He wrapped it in a sheet of newspaper, dropped the package into a string bag and went again downstairs, wearing sockless sandals, tight trousers, and black beret. Sometimes he wore sunglasses.

At the corner he stepped into midstreet, repelled by the old crone's door, the fortune-teller, the eighth of seven sisters to hear her talk, six thick hairs sprouting from the wart on her chin; in order not to sneak in and ask, for one hundred lire, 'Tell me, signora, will I ever make it? Will I finish my five years' painting of Mother and Son? my sure masterpiece – I know it in my bones – if I ever get it done.'

Her shrill sibyllic reply made sense. 'A good cook doesn't throw out yesterday's soup.'

'But will it be as good, I mean? Very good, signora, maybe a masterwork?'

'Masters make masterworks.'

'And what about my luck, when will it change from the usual?'

'When you do. Art is long, inspiration, short. Luck is fine, but don't stop breathing.'

'Will I avoid an unhappy fate?'

'It all depends.'

That or something like it for one hundred lire. No bargain.

F sighed. Still, it somehow encouraged.

A window shutter was drawn up with a clatter and a paper cone of garbage came flying out at him. He ducked as the oily bag split on the cobblestones behind him.

BEWARE OF FALLING MASONRY.

He turned the corner, barely avoiding three roaring Vespas.

Vita pericolosa. It had been a suffocating summer slowly deflated to cool autumn. He hurried, not to worry his hunger, past the fruit and vegetable stalls in the piazza, zigzagging through the Oltrarno streets as he approached Ponte Vecchio. Ah, the painter's eye! He enjoyed the narrow crowded noisy streets, the washing hung from windows. Tourists were all but gone, but the workshops were preparing for next year's migration, mechanics assembling picture frames, cutting leather, plastering tile mosaics; women plaiting straw. He sneezed passing through a tannery reek followed by hot stink of stable. Above the din of traffic an old forge rumbling. F hastened by a minuscule gallery where one of his action paintings had been hanging downside up for more than a year. He had made no protest, art lives on accidents.

At a small square, thick with stone benches where before the war there had been houses, the old and lame of the quarter sat amid beggars and berouged elderly whores, one near by combing her reddish-grey locks. Another fed pigeons with a crust of bread they approached and pecked at. One, not so old, in a homely floppy velvet hat, he gazed at twice; in fact no more than a girl with a slender youthful body. He could stand a little sexual comfort but it cost too much. Holding the Madonna tightly to his chest, the painter hastened into the woodworker's shop.

Alberto Panenero, the proprietor, in a brown smock

smeared with wood dust and shavings, scattered three apprentices with a hiss and came forward, bowing.

'Ah, maestro, another of your charming Madonnas, let's hope?'

F unwrapped the wooden statuette of the modest Madonna.

The proprietor held it up as he examined it. He called together the apprentices. 'Look at the workmanship, you ignoramuses,' then dismissed them with a hiss.

'Beautiful?' F said.

'Of course. With that subject who can miss?'

'And the price?'

'Eh. What can one do? As usual.'

F's face fell an inch. 'Is it fair to pay only five thousand lire for a statuette that takes two weeks' work and sells on Via Tornabuoni for fifteen thousand, even twenty if someone takes it to St Peter's and gets it blessed by the Pope?'

Panenero shrugged: 'Ah, maestro, the world has changed since the time of true craftsmen. You and I we're fighting a losing battle. As for the Madonnas, I now get most of the job turned out by machine. My apprentices cut in the face, add a few folds to the robe, daub on a bit of paint, and I swear to you it costs me one third of what I pay you and goes for the same price to the shops. Of course, they don't approach the quality of your product – I'm an honest man – but do you think the tourists care? What's more the shopkeepers are stingier than ever, and believe me they're stingy in Florence. If I ask for more they offer less. If they pay me seventy-five hundred for yours I'm in luck. With that price, how can I take care of rent and my other expenses? I pay the wages of two masters and a journeyman on my other products, the antique furniture and so forth. I also employ three apprentices who have to eat or they're too weak to fart. My own family, including a clubfoot son and three useless daughters, comes to six people. Eh, I don't have to tell you it's no picnic earning a living nowadays. Still, if you'll put a bambino in the poor Madonna's arms, I'll up you five hundred.'

'I'll take the five thousand.'

The proprietor counted it out in worn fifty- and one hundred-lire notes.

'The trouble with you, maestro, is you're a perfectionist. How many are there nowadays?'

'I guess that's so,' F sighed. 'Don't think I haven't thought of selling the Madonnas to the tourists myself, but if I have to do that as well as make them where's my painting time coming from, I'd like to know?'

'I agree with you totally,' Panenero said, 'still, for a bachelor you're not doing too badly. I'm always surprised you look so skinny. It must be hereditary.'

'Most of my earnings go for supplies. Everything's shot up so, oils, pigments, turpentine, everything. A tube of cadmium costs close to thirteen hundred lire, so I try to keep bright yellow, not to mention vermilion, out of my pictures. Last week I had to pass up a sable brush they ask three thousand for. A roll of cotton canvas costs over ten thousand. With such prices what's left for meat?'

'Too much meat is bad for the digestion. My wife's brother eats meat twice a day and has liver trouble. A dish of good spaghetti with cheese will fatten you up without interfering with your liver. Anyway how's the painting coming?'

'Don't ask me so I won't lie.'

In the market close by, F pinched the tender parts of two Bosc pears and a Spanish melon. He looked into a basket of figs, examined some pumpkins on hooks, inspected a bleeding dead rabbit and told himself he must do a couple of still lifes. He settled for a long loaf of bread and two etti of tripe. He also bought a brown egg for breakfast, six Nazionale cigarettes and a quarter of a head of cabbage. In a fit of well-being he bought three wine-red dahlias, and the old woman who sold them to him out of her basket handed him a marigold, free. Shopping for food's a blessing, he thought, you get down to brass tacks. It makes a lot in life seem less important, for instance painting a masterwork. He felt he needn't paint for the rest of his life and nothing much lost; but then anxiety moved like a current through his belly as the thought threatened and he had all he could do not to break into a sweat, run back to the studio, set up his canvas and start hitting it with paint. I'm a time-ravaged man, horrible curse on an artist.

The young whore with the baggy hat saw the flowers amid his bundles as he approached, and through her short veil smiled dimly up at him.

F, for no reason he could think of, gave her the marigold, and the girl – she was no more than eighteen – held the flower awkwardly.

'What's your price, if you don't mind me asking?'

'What are you, a painter or something?'

'That's right, how did you know?'

'I think I guessed. Maybe it's your clothes, or the flowers or something.' She smiled absently, her eyes roaming the benches, her hard mouth tight. 'To answer your question, two thousand lire.'

He raised his beret and walked on.

'You can have me for five hundred,' called an old whore from her bench. 'What she hasn't heard of I've practiced all my life. I have no objection to odd requests.'

But F was running. Got to get back to work. He crossed

91

the street through a flood of Fiats, carts, Vespas, and rushed
back to his studio.

Afterwards he sat on his bed, hands clasped between knees,
looking at the canvas and thinking of the young whore.
Maybe it'd relax me so I can paint.

He counted what was left of his money, then hid the
paper lire in a knotted sock in his bureau drawer. He removed the sock and hid it in the armadio on the hat rack.
Then he locked the armadio and hid the key in the bureau
drawer. He dropped the drawer key into a jar of cloudy
turpentine, figuring who would want to wet his hand fishing
for it.

Maybe she'd let me charge it and I could pay when I
have more money? I could do two Madonnas sometime
and pay her out of the ten thousand lire.

Then he thought. She seemed interested in me as an
artist. Maybe she'd trade for a drawing.

He riffled through a pile of charcoal drawings and came
on one of a heavy-bellied nude cutting her toenails, one
chunky foot on a backless chair. F trotted to the benches
in the market piazza where the girl sat with a crushed marigold in her hand.

'Would you mind having a drawing instead? One of my
own, that is?'

'Instead of what?'

'Instead of cash because I'm short. It's just a thought I
had.'

It took her a minute to run it through her head. 'All
right, if that's what you want.'

He unrolled the drawing and showed it to her.

'Oh, all right.'

But then she flushed under her veil and gazed embarrassed at F.

'Anything wrong?'

Her eyes miserably searched the piazza.

'It's nothing,' she said after a minute. 'I'll take your drawing.' Then seeing him studying her she laughed nervously and said, 'I was looking for my cousin. He's supposed to meet me here. Well, if he comes let him wait, he's a pain in the ass anyway.'

She rose from the bench and they went together towards Via S. Agostino.

Fabio, the landlord, took one look and called her puttana.

'That'll do from you,' said F, sternly.

'Pay your rent instead of pissing away the money.'

Her name, she told him as they were undressing in his studio, was Esmeralda.

His was Arturo.

The girl's hair, when she tossed off her baggy hat, was brown and full. She had black eyes like plum pits, a small mouth on the sad side, Modigliani neck, strong though not exactly white teeth and a pimply brow. She wore long imitation-pearl ear-rings and kept them on. Esmeralda unzipped her clothes and they were at once in bed. It wasn't bad though she apologized for her performance.

As they lay smoking in bed – he had given her one of his six cigarettes – Esmeralda said, 'The one I was looking for isn't my cousin, he's my pimp or at least he was. If he's there waiting for me I hope it's a blizzard and he freezes to death.'

They had an espresso together. She said she liked the studio and offered to stay.

He was momentarily panicked. 'I wouldn't want it to interfere with my painting. I mean I'm devoted to that. Besides, this is a small place.'

93

'I'm a small girl, I'll take care of your needs and won't interfere with your work.'

He finally agreed.

Though he had qualms concerning her health, he let her stay yet felt reasonably contented.

'Il Signor Ludovico Belvedere,' the landlord called up from the ground floor, 'a gentleman on his way up the stairs to see you. If he buys one of your pictures, you won't have any excuse for not paying last month's rent, not to mention June or July.'

If it was really a gentleman, F went in to wash his hands as the stranger slowly, stopping to breathe, wound his way up the stairs. The painter had hastily removed the canvas from the easel, hiding it in the kitchen alcove. He soaped his hands thickly, the smoke from the butt in his mouth drifting into a closed eye. F quickly dried himself with a dirty towel. It was, instead of a gentleman, Esmeralda's seedy cugino, the pimp, a thin man past fifty, tall, with pouched small eyes and a pencil-line moustache. His hands and feet were small, he wore loose squeaky shoes with grey spats. His clothes though neatly pressed had seen better days. He carried a malacca cane and sported a pearl-grey hat. There was about him, though he seemed to mask it, a quality of having experienced everything, if not more, that gave F the momentary shivers.

Bowing courteously and speaking as though among friends, he was not, he explained, in the best of moods – to say nothing of his health – after a week of running around desperately trying to locate Esmeralda. He explained they had had a misunderstanding over a few lire through an unfortunate error, no more than a mistake in addition – carrying a one instead of a seven. 'These things happen to the best of mathematicians, but what can you do with someone who won't listen to reason? She slapped my face and ran off. Through a mutual acquaintance I made an appointment to explain the matter to her, with proof from my accounts, but though she gave her word she didn't appear. It doesn't speak well for her maturity.'

He had learned later from a friend in the Santo Spirito quarter that she was at the moment living with the signore. Ludovico apologized for disturbing him, but F must understand he had come out of urgent necessity.

'Per piacere, signore, I request your good will. A great deal is at stake for four people. She can continue to serve you from time to time if that's what she wants; but I hear from your landlord that you're not exactly prosperous, and on the other hand she has to support herself and a starving father in Fiesole. I don't suppose she's told you about him but if it weren't for me personally, he'd be lying in a common grave this minute growing flowers on his chest. She must come back to work under my guidance and protection not only because it's mutually beneficial but because it's a matter of communal responsibility; not only hers for me now that I've had a most serious operation, or both of us for her starving father, but also in reference to my aged mother, a woman of eighty-three who is seriously in need of proper nursing care. I understand you're an American, signore. That's one thing but Italy is a poor country. Here each of us is responsible for the welfare of four or five others or we all go under.'

He spoke calmly, philosophically, occasionally breathlessly, as if his recent operation now and then caught up with him. And his intense small eyes wandered in different directions as he talked, as though he suspected Esmeralda might be hiding.

F, after his first indignation, listened with interest although disappointed the man had not turned out to be a wealthy picture buyer.

'She's had it with whoring,' he said.

'Signore,' Ludovico answered with emotion, 'it's important to understand. The girl owes me much. She was seventeen when I came across her, a peasant girl living a wretched existence. I'll spare you the details because they'd turn your stomach. She had chosen this profession, the most difficult of all as we both know, but lacked the ability to handle herself. I met her by accident and offered to help her although this sort of thing wasn't in my regular line of work. To make the story short, I devoted many hours to her education and found her a better clientele – to give you an example, recently one of her newest customers, a rich cripple she sees every week, offered to marry her, but I advised against it because he's a contadino. I also took measures to protect her health and well-being. I advised her to go for periodic medical examinations, scared off badly behaved customers with a toy pistol, and tried in every way to reduce indignities and hazards. Believe me, I am a protective person and gave her my sincere affection. I treat her as if she were my own daughter. She isn't by chance in the next room? Why doesn't she come out and talk frankly?'

He pointed with his cane at the alcove curtain.

'That's the kitchen,' said F. 'She's at the market.'

Ludovico, bereft, blew on his fingers, his eyes momentarily glazed as his glance mechanically wandered around the room. He seemed then to come to and gazed at some of F's pictures with interest. In a moment his features were animated.

'Naturally, you're a painter! Pardon me for overlooking

it, a worried man is half blind. Besides, somebody said you were an insurance agent.'

'No, I'm a painter.'

The pimp borrowed F's last cigarette, took a few puffs as he studied the pictures on the wall with tightened eyes, then put out the barely-used butt and pocketed it.

'It's a remarkable coincidence.' He had once, it turned out, been a frame maker and later part-owner of a small art gallery on Via Strozzi, and he was of course familiar with painting and the painting market. But the gallery, because of the machinations of his thieving partner, had failed. He hadn't re-opened it for lack of capital. It was shortly afterwards he had had to have a lung removed.

'That's why I didn't finish your cigarette.'

Ludovico coughed badly – F believed him.

'In this condition, naturally, I find it difficult to make a living. Even frame making wears me out. That's why it's advantageous for me to work with Esmeralda.'

'Anyway, you certainly have your nerve,' the painter replied. 'I'm not just referring to your coming up here and telling me what I ought to do vis-à-vis someone who happens to be here because she asked to be, but I mean actually living off the proceeds of a girl's body. All in all, it isn't much of a moral thing to do. Esmeralda might in some ways be indebted to you but she doesn't owe you her soul.'

The pimp leaned with dignity on his cane.

'Since you bring up the word, signore, are you a moral man?'

'In my art I am.'

Ludovico sighed. 'Ah, maestro, who are we to talk of what we understand so badly? Morality has a thousand sources and endless means of expression. As for the soul, who understands its mechanism? Remember, the thief on the cross was the one who rose to heaven with Our Lord.' He coughed at length. 'Keep in mind that the girl of her free will chose her calling, not I. She was in it without finesse or proficiency, although she is of course adequate. Her advantage is her youth and a certain directness but she needs advice and managerial assistance. Have you seen the hat she wears? Twice I tried to burn it. Obviously she lacks taste. The same is true for her clothes but she's very stubborn to deal with. Still, I devote myself to her and manage to improve conditions, for which I receive a modest but necessary commission. Considering the circumstances, how can this be an evil thing? The basis of morality is recognizing one another's needs and cooperating. Mutual generosity is nothing to criticize other people for. After all, what did Jesus teach?'

Ludovico had removed his hat. He was bald with several grey hairs parted in the centre.

He seemed, now, depressed. 'You aren't in love with her, are you, maestro? If so, say the word and I disappear. Love is love, after all. I don't forget I'm an Italian.'

F thought for a minute.

'Not as yet, I don't think.'

'In that case I hope you will not interfere with her decision?'

'What decision do you have in mind?'

'As to what she will do after I speak to her.'

'You mean if she decides to leave?'

'Exactly.'

'That's up to her.'

The pimp ran a relieved hand over his perspiring head and replaced his hat. 'The relationship may be momentarily convenient, but for a painter who has his work to think of you'll be better off without her.'

'I didn't say I wanted her to go,' said F. 'All I said was I wouldn't interfere with her decision.'

Ludovico bowed. 'Ah, you have the objectivity of a true artist.'

On his way out, he tossed aside the alcove curtain with his cane and uncovered F's painting on the kitchen table.

He seemed at first unable to believe his eyes. Standing back, he had a better look. 'Straordinario,' he murmured, kissing his fingertips.

F snatched the canvas, blew off the dust and carefully tucked it behind his bureau.

'It's work in progress,' he explained. 'I don't like to show it yet.'

'Obviously it will be a very fine painting, one sees that at a glance. What do you call it?'

"'Mother and Son.'"

'In spirit it's pure Picasso.'

'Is it?'

'I refer to his remark: "You paint not what you see but what you know is there."'

'That's right,' F said, his voice husky.

'We all have to learn from the masters. There's nothing wrong with trying to do better that which they do best themselves. Thus new masters are born.'

'Thank you.'

'When you finish let me know. I am acquainted with people who are interested in buying fine serious contemporary work. I could get you an excellent price, of course for the usual commission. Anyway, it looks as though you are about to give birth to a painting of extraordinary merit. Permit me to congratulate you on your talent.'

F blushed radiantly.

Esmeralda returned.

Ludovico fell to his knees.

'Go fuck yourself,' she said.

'Ah, signorina, my misfortune is your good luck. Your friend is a superb artist. You can take my word for it.'

How do you paint a Kaddish?

Here's Momma sitting on the stoop in her cotton house-dress, awkward at having her picture taken yet with a dim smile on the dry old snapshot turning yellow that Bessie sent me years ago. Here's the snap, here's the painting of the same idea, why can't I make one out of both? How do you make art of an old photo, so to say? A single of a double image, the one in and the one out?

The painting, 51×38, was encrusted in places (her hands and feet) (his face) almost a quarter of an inch thick with paint, layer on layer giving it history, another word for thick past in the paint itself. The mastery was why in the five years he had been at it, on and off because he had to hide it away when it got to be too much for him, he hadn't been able to finish it though most of it was done already, except Momma's face. Five years' work here, mostly as he had first painted it, though he often added dibs and dabs, touches of brush or palette knife on the dry forms. He had tried it every which way, with Momma alone, sitting or standing, with or without him; and with Bessie in or out, but never Poppa, that living ghost; and I've made her old and young, and sometimes resembling Annamaria Oliovino, or Teresa, the chambermaid in Milan; even a little like Susskind, when my memory gets mixed up, who was a man I met when I first came to Rome. Momma apart and him apart, and then trying to bring them together in the tightly woven paint so they would be eternally mother and son as well as unique forms on canvas. So beautifully complete the idea of them together that the viewer couldn't help but think no one has to do it again because it's been done by F and can't be done better; in truth, a masterwork. He had painted her sad and happy, tall, short, realistic, expressionistic, cubistic, surrealistic, even in action splotches of violet and brown. Also in black and white, stark like Kline or Motherwell. Once he had moulded a figure in clay from the old photo and tried to copy it, but that didn't work either.

The faces were changed almost every day he painted, his as a young boy, hers as herself (long since departed); but now though for a year he had let the boy be, his face and all, he was still never satisfied with hers – something always missing – for very long after he had put it down; and he daily or nightly scraped it off (another lost face) with his rusty palette knife, and tried once again the next day; then scraped that face the same night or the day after; or let it harden in hope for two days and then frantically before the paint stiffened, scraped that face off, too. All in all he had destroyed more than a thousand faces and conceived another thousand for a woman who could barely afford one; yet couldn't settle on her true face – at least true for art. What was true for Bessie's old photo was true enough – you can't beat Kodak, but reduced on canvas, too much omitted. He sometimes thought of tearing up the old snapshot so he would have only memory (of it?) to go by, but couldn't bring himself to destroy this last image of her. He was afraid to tear up the snap and went on painting the face on the dumpy body on the chair on the stoop, little F standing blandly by her side knowing she had died though pretending, at least in paint, that he didn't; then scraping it off as the rest of the painting slowly thickened into a frieze.

I've caught the boy, more or less, and sometimes I seem

to have her for a few minutes, though not when I look at them together. I don't paint her face so that it holds him in her presence. It comes out at best like two portraits in space and time. Should I stand him on the left instead of right? I tried it once and it didn't work; now I have this hard-as-rock-quarter-of-an-inch investment in the way they are now, and if I scrap either of them (chisel? dynamite?), I might as well throw out the canvas. I might as well scrap what's left of my life if I have to start over again.

How do you invent whoever she was? I remember so little, her death, not even the dying, just the end mostly, after a sickness they easily cure nowadays with penicillin. I was about six or seven, or maybe ten, and as I remember, didn't cry at the funeral. For years that never bothered me much, but when Bessie sent me the snap and I began painting Momma's pictures, I guess it did. Maybe I held it against her, I mean dying; either that or I am by nature a non-mourner, born that way whether one wants it or not. The truth is I am afraid to paint, like I might find out something about myself.

I have not said Kaddish, though I could have looked up the words.

What if she were still a wandering figure among the stars, unable to find the Pearly Gates?

He hid the canvas and turned then to the statuette of the Madonna without child. Esmeralda liked to see the chips fly as the Holy Mother rose out of wood.

The girl had coffee with milk in the morning, slept on a borrowed cot in the kitchen alcove and stayed out of his way while he was painting. The back of the canvas was what she saw when she came into the studio each morning for a few lire to shop with. It was understood she was not to try to look as he painted. 'Malocchio,' he said, and she nodded and withdrew on tiptoe. Because he found it uncomfortable to work with someone around, after a few days he had thought of asking her to leave, but when he considered how young she was, hardly grown up, like a young child's big sister, he changed his mind. Only once she indirectly referred to the painting, asking what was the snapshot he pored over so much. 'Mind your business,' F said; she shrugged and withdrew. In the kitchen she was slowly reading a love serial in a movie magazine. She shopped, cooked, kept the studio clean, although she did not bathe as often as he. In the kitchen, as he painted, she mended his socks and underwear, and altered her dresses. She had not much clothing, a sweater and skirt and two trollop's dresses, from one of which she removed two silver roses, from the other some rows of purple sequins. She sewed up the necklines and lowered the hems. She owned a tight black sweater that looked good on her because of her healthy bosom, long neck, dark eyes; also a few pieces of patched underwear, nothing enticing but a red chemise, not bad but too red, some baubles of jewellery she had bought on the Ponte Vecchio, and a modest pair of house shoes. Her gold high heels she had wrapped in newspaper and put away. How long for does she think? F thought. And the girl was a talented cook. She fed him well, mostly on macaroni, green vegetables cooked in olive oil, and now and then some tripe or rabbit. She did very well with a few lire, and all in all two lived cheaper than one. She made no complaints, though she could be sullen when, lost in his work or worry, he paid scant attention to her for days. She obliged in bed when he wanted her, could be tender, and generally made herself useful. Esmeralda once suggested she would pose for him in the nude but F wouldn't hear of it. Heavy-armed and long-footed, at times she reminded him of Bessie as a girl, though they weren't really much alike.

One October morning F sprang out of bed, terribly inspired. Before breakfast he got the painting out of its hiding place to finish off once and for all, only to discover that Bessie's snapshot was gone from the easel ledge. He shook Esmeralda awake but she hadn't seen it. F rushed downstairs, dumped the garbage bag on the sidewalk and frantically searched amid the hard spaghetti strings and mushy melon rinds, as the landlord waving both arms threatened suit. No luck. Upstairs, he hunted through the studio from top to bottom, Esmeralda diligently assisting, but they found nothing. He spent a terrible morning, not a stroke painted.

'But why do you need a picture to paint from, it's all so ridiculous.'

'Are you sure you didn't take it?'

'Why would I take it? It's not a picture of me.'

'To teach me a lesson or something?'

'Don't be a fool,' she said.

He trembled in rage and misery.

In his presence she searched through his chest of drawers – he had been through them a dozen times – and on top, under a book on Uccello he had been reading, discovered the lost snap.

F blushed.

'I forgive your dirty suspicions,' she said, her eyes clouding.

'Not that I deserve it,' he admitted.

After lunch she tried on the floppy hat she had worn when he met her, to see how she could alter it.

The sight of the velvet hat on her excited his eye. F had another inspiration.

'I'll paint you in it – at least a drawing.'

'What for? You said it's ugly on me.'

'It's unique is why. Many a master in the past was enticed by a hat to do a portrait of the face beneath. Rembrandt, for instance.'

'Oh, all right,' Esmeralda said. 'It's immaterial to me. I thought you'd want to be getting back to your painting.'

'The day's shot for that.'

She agreed to pose. He did a quick charcoal for a warm-up that came out entrancing, especially the hat. He began then to sketch her in pencil, possibly for a painting.

As he was drawing, F asked, 'How did you happen to fall into prosti – your former profession? What I mean is, was it Ludovico's doing?'

'Prosti – profession,' she mimicked. 'Once you've cackled, lay the egg.'

'I was trying to be considerate.'

'Try again. Keeping your mouth shut about certain things is a better consideration; still, if it's only your curiosity you're out to satisfy, I'll tell you why. Ludovico had nothing to do with it, at least then, although he was one of my earliest customers and still owes me money for services rendered, not to mention certain sums he stole outright. He's the only pure bastard I know, all the others have strains of decency, not that it makes much difference. Anyway, it was my own idea, if you want to know. Maybe I was working up to be an artist's mistress.'

F, letting the sarcasm pass, continued to sketch her.

'One thing I'll tell you, it wasn't because of any starving father, if that's what he's told you. My father has a tiny farm in Fiesole, he stinks of manure and is incredibly stingy. All he's ever parted with is his virginity. He's got my mother and sister drudging for him and is sore as a castrated bull that I escaped. I ran away because I was sick to my teeth of being a slave. What's more, he wasn't above giving me a feel now and then when he had nothing better to do. Thanks to him I can barely read and write. I turned to whoring because I don't want to be a maid and I don't know anything else. A truck driver on the autostrada gave me the idea. But in spite of my profession I'm incredibly shy, that's why I let Ludovico pimp for me.'

She asked if she could see the drawing of herself, and when she had, said, 'What are you going to call it?'

He had thought, 'Portrait of a Young Whore', but answered, '"Portrait of a Young Woman". I might do an oil from it.'

'It's immaterial to me,' Esmeralda said, but she was pleased.

'The reason I stayed here is I thought you'd be kind to me. Besides, if a man is an artist I figured he must know about life. If he does maybe he can teach me something. So far all I've learned is you're like everybody else, shivering in your drawers. That's how it goes, when you think you have nothing there's somebody with less.'

F made three more drawings on paper, with and without the hat, and one with the black hat and Esmeralda holding marigolds.

The next morning he carved half a wooden Madonna in a few hours, and to celebrate, took Esmeralda to the Uffizi in the afternoon and explained some of the great works of art to her.

She didn't always understand his allusions but was grateful. 'You're not so dumb,' she said.

'One picks up things.'

That evening they went to a movie and afterwards stopped for a gelato in a café off the Piazza della Signoria. Men looked over her. F stared them down. She smiled at him tenderly. 'You're a lot more relaxed when you're working on the Madonnas. When you're painting with that snapshot in front of you, you haven't the civility of a dog.'

He admitted the truth of it.

She confessed she had stolen a long look at his painting when he was downstairs going through the garbage bag for the snap.

To his surprise he did not condemn her.

'What did you think of it?'

'Who is she, the one without the face?'

'My mother, she died young.'

'What's the matter with the boy?'

'What do you mean?'

'He looks kind of sad.'

'That's the way it's supposed to be. But I don't want to talk about it. That can ruin the painting.'

'To me it's as though you were trying to paint yourself into your mother's arms.'

He was momentarily stunned. 'Do you think so?'

'It's obvious to me. A mother's a mother, a son's a son.'

'True, but it might be like an attempt on my part to release her from the arms of death. But that sort of stuff doesn't matter much. It's first and foremost a painting, potentially a first-class work if I ever get it done. If I could complete it the way I sometimes see it in my mind's eye, I bet it could be something extraordinary. If a man does only one such painting in his lifetime, he can call himself a success. I sometimes think that if I could paint such a picture, much that was wrong in my life would rearrange itself and add up to more, if you know what I mean.'

'In what way?'

'I could forgive myself for past errors.'

'Not me,' Esmeralda said. 'I'd have to paint ten great pictures.' She laughed at the thought.

As they were crossing the bridge, Esmeralda said, 'You're really nutty. I don't see why a man would give up five years of his life just to paint one picture. If it was me I'd put it aside and do something I could sell.'

'I do once in a while, like this portrait of you I'm working on now, but I always go back to "Mother and Son".'

'Why does everybody talk about art so much?' she asked. 'Even Ludovico, when he's not adding up his accounts, he's talking about art.'

'Art's what it must be, which is beauty, and more, which is mostly mystery. That's what people talk about.'

'In this picture you're painting of me, what's the mystery?'

'The mystery is you've been captured, yet there's more – you've become art.'

'You mean it's not me any more?'

'It never was. Art isn't life.'

'Then the hell with it. If I have my choice I'll take life. If there's not that there's no art.'

'Without art there's no life to speak of, at least for me. If I'm not an artist, then I'm nothing.'

'My God, aren't you a man?'

'Not really, without art.'

'Personally, I think you have a lot to learn.'

'I'm learning,' F sighed.

'What's so great about mystery?' she asked. 'I don't like it. There's enough around without making more.'

'Being involved in it.'

'Explain that to me.'

'It's complicated, but one thing would be that a man like

108

me – you understand – is actually working in art. The idea came to me late, I wasted most of my youth. The mystery of art is that more is there than you put down and every stroke adds to it. You look at your painting and see this bull's-eye staring at you though all you've painted is an old tree. It's also a mystery to me why I haven't been able to finish my best painting though I am dying to.'

'If you ask me,' Esmeralda said, 'my idea of a mystery is why I am in love with you, though it's clear to me you don't see me for dirt.'

She burst into tears.

A week later Ludovico, come for a morning visit wearing new yellow gloves, saw the completed portrait of Esmeralda, 48 × 30, with black hat, long neck, and marigolds. He was bowled over.

'Fantastic. If you pay me half, I can get you a million lire for this work of art.'

F agreed, so the pimp, crossing himself, left with the painting.

One afternoon when Esmeralda was out, Ludovico, breathing badly after four flights of stairs, appeared in the studio lugging a tape recorder he had borrowed for an interview with F.

'What for?'

'To keep a record for the future. I'll get it printed in *International Arts*. My cousin is assistant to the business manager. I will help you get a gallery for your first one-man show.'

'Who needs a gallery if all I can show is unfinished canvases?'

'You'd better increase your output. Sit down here and talk into the microphone. I've turned it on. Don't worry about the machine, it won't crawl up your leg. Just relax and answer my questions candidly. Also, don't waste time justifying yourself. Are you ready?'

'Yes.'

LUD : Very well. Ludovico Belvedere speaking, interviewing the painter Fidelman. Tell me, Arturo, as an American what does painting mean to you?

F : It's my whole life.

LUD : What kind of person do you think an artist is when he's painting? Do you think he's a king or an emperor, or a seer or prophet?

F : I don't know for sure. I often feel like a constipated witch doctor.

LUD : Please talk with good sense. If you're going to be scatological I'll stop the machine.

F : I didn't mean anything bad.

LUD : As an American painter, what do you think of Jackson Pollock? Do you agree that he is a liberating influence?

F : I guess so. The truth is you have to liberate yourself.

LUD : We're talking about painting, not your personal psychology. Jackson Pollock, as any cultured person will tell you, has changed the course of modern painting. Don't think we don't know about him in this country, we're not exactly backward. We can all learn from him, including you. Do you agree that anyone who works in the modes of the past has only leavings to work with?

F : Only partly, the past is pretty rich.

LUD : I go now to the next question. Who is your favourite painter?

F : Ah – well, I don't think I have one, I have many.

LUD : If you think that's an advantage, you're wrong.

There's no need of hubris. If an interviewer asked me that question, I would reply 'Leonardo, Raphael, Michelangelo', or someone else but not the entire pantheon of painters.

F: I answered honestly.

LUD: Anyway, to go on, what is your avowed purpose in art?

F: To do the best I can. To do more than that. My momentary purpose is to create my uncreated masterpiece.

LUD: The one of your mother?

F: That's right, 'Mother and Son'.

LUD: But where is your originality? Why are you so concerned with subject matter?

F: I reject originality.

LUD: What's that? Please explain yourself.

F: Maybe I'm not ready, not just yet.

LUD: Mother of God! How old are you?

F: About forty. A little more.

LUD: But why are you so cautious and conservative? I'm fifty-two and have the mind of a youth. Tell me, what's your opinion of pop art? Think before you speak.

F: If it stays away from me, I'll stay away from it.

LUD: (garbled)

F: What did you say?

LUD: Please attend to the question at hand. I wish you would explain to me clearly why you paint.

F: With my paintings I try to stop the flow of time.

LUD: That's a ridiculous statement, but go on anyway.

F: I've said it.

LUD: Say it more comprehensibly. The public will read this.

F: Well, art is my means for understanding life and

trying out certain assumptions I have. I make art, it makes me.

LUD : We have a proverb: 'The bray of an ass can't be heard in heaven.'

F : Frankly, I don't care for some of your remarks.

LUD : Are you saying the canvas is the alter ego of the artist's miserable self?

F : That's not what I said and I don't like what you're saying.

LUD : I'll try to be more respectful. Maestro, once you spoke to me of your art as moral. What did you mean by that?

F : It's just a thought I had, I guess. I suppose I mean that maybe a painting sort of gives value to a human being as he responds to it. You might say it enlarges his consciousness. If he feels beauty it makes him more than he was, it adds, you might say, to his humanity.

LUD : What do you mean 'responds'? A man responds in rape, doesn't he? Doesn't that enlarge the consciousness, as you put it?

F : It's a different response. Rape isn't art.

LUD : An emotion is an emotion, no matter how it arises. In itself it is not moral or immoral. Suppose someone responds to the sunset on the Arno? Is that better or more moral than the response to the smell of a drowned corpse? What about bad art? Suppose the response is with more feeling than to a great painting – does that prove bad art is moral, as you call it?

F : I guess not. All right, maybe the painting itself doesn't have it, but putting it another way, maybe the artist does; that is he does when he's painting – creating form, order. Order protects us all, doesn't it?

112

LUD: Yes, the way a prison does. Remember, some of the biggest pricks, if you will excuse the use of this word, have been great painters. Does that necessarily make them moral men? Of course not. What if a painter kills his father and then paints a beautiful Ascension?

F: Maybe I'm not putting it exactly right. Maybe what I'm trying to say is that I feel most moral when I'm painting, like being engaged with truth.

LUD: So now it's what you feel. I speak with respect, maestro, but you do nothing but assault me with garbage.

F: Look, Ludovico, I don't understand, if you don't mind my saying so, why you brought this machine up here if all you want to do is insult me. Now take it away, it's using up work-time.

LUD: I am not a servant, maestro. I may have been forced into menial work through circumstance, but Ludovico Belvedere has kept his dignity. Don't think that because you are an American you can go on trampling on the rights of Europeans. You have caused me unnecessary personal discomfort and sorrow by interfering in a business relationship between this unfortunate girl and myself, and the lives of four people have been seriously affected. You don't seem to realize the harm you are doing—

END OF INTERVIEW.

F had assaulted the tape recorder.

Each morning he awoke earlier to paint, waiting for dawn though the light from the streaked sky was, of course, impossible. He had lately been capable of very little patience with the necessities of daily life; to wash, dress, eat, even go to the toilet; and the matter became most inconvenient when his nervous impatience seeped into painting itself. It was a burdensome business to take the canvas out of its hiding place behind the armadio and arrange it on the easel, select and mix his paints, tack up the old snapshot (most unbearable) and begin work. He could have covered the canvas on the easel at night and left the snapshot tacked on permanently, but was obsessed to remove it each time after he put the paints away, soaked his brushes in turpentine, cleaned up. Formerly, just picking up a brush and standing in thought, or reverie, or sometimes blankly, before painting, would ease interior constrictions to the point where he could relax sufficiently to enjoy the work; and once he had painted for an hour, which sometimes came to no more than a stroke or two, he felt well enough to permit himself to eat half a roll and swallow an espresso Esmeralda had prepared, and afterwards go with lit butt and magazine to the gabinetto. But now there were days he stood in terror before 'Mother and Son' and shivered with every stroke he put down.

He painted out of anguish, a dark colour. The canvas remained much the same, the boy as he had been, the fickle mother's face daily changing; daily he scraped it off as Esmeralda moaned in the kitchen; she knew the sound of palette knife on canvas. It was then it occurred to F to use the girl as a model for his mother. Though she was only eighteen, it might help to have a living model for Momma as a young woman though she was touching middle age when Bessie took the photo, and was of course another sort of person; still, such were the paradoxes of art. Esmeralda agreed and stripped herself to the skin, but the painter sternly ordered her to dress; it was her face he was painting. She did as he demanded and patiently posed, sweetly, absently, uncomplaining, for hours, as he, fighting against his need for privacy in the creative art, tried anew to invent the mother's face. I've done all I can with imagination, I mean on top of the snapshot. And though at the end of the day he scraped her face off as the model wept, F urged her to be calm because he now had a brand-new idea: to paint himself not with Momma any more but Bessie instead, 'Brother and Sister'. Esmeralda's face lit up because 'then you'll stop using the snapshot'. But F replied, 'Not exactly', he still needed it to get the true relationship of them 'in space as well as psychology'.

As they were into the spaghetti at supper, the girl wanted to know if all artists had it so hard.

'How hard?'

'So that it takes them years to paint a picture?'

'Some do and some don't. What's on your mind?'

'Oh, I don't know,' she said.

He slammed down his fork. 'Are you doubting my talent, you whore?'

She got up and went into the gabinetto.

F lay on his bed, his face engulfed in a pillowful of black thoughts.

After a while Esmeralda came out and kissed his ear.

'I forgive you, tesoro, I want you to succeed.'

'I will,' he cried, springing up from the bed.

The next day he rigged up a young boy's costume – blouse and knee pants, and painted in it to get to the heart of bygone days, but that didn't work either so he went back to putting Esmeralda into the painting and scraping her face off each night.

To live, to paint, to live to paint he had to continue carving Madonnas; being impatient he made them more reluctantly. When Esmeralda pointed out they had some sauce but no spaghetti, in three days he hurried out a statuette then hurried it over to Panenero's shop. The woodworker unfortunately couldn't use it. 'My apprentices,' he shrugged, 'are turning them out by the barrelful. Frankly, they model each stroke on yours and work fast. Eh, that's what happens to craft in these times. So the stuff piles up and the tourists won't be here till spring. It's a long time till the hackensacks and lederhosen come over the Alps, maestro. Still, because it's you and I admire your skill, I'll offer you two thousand lire, take it or leave it. This is my busy day.'

F left without a word, in afterthought wondering whose yellow gloves he had seen lying on the counter. On his way along the riverbank he flung the Madonna into the Arno. She struck the green water with a golden splash, sank, then rose to the surface, and turning on her back, floated downstream, eyes to the blue sky.

He later carved two more Madonnas, finely wrought pieces, and peddled them himself to shops on the Vie Tornabuoni and della Vigna Nuova. No luck. The shelves were crammed full of religious figures, though one of the merchants offered him six thousand lire for a Marilyn Monroe, nude if possible.

'I have no skill for that sort of thing.'

'What about John the Baptist in shaggy skins?'

'What about him?'

'I offer five thousand.'

'I find him an uninteresting figure.'

Esmeralda then tried selling the statuettes. F wouldn't let her offer them to Panenero, so the girl, holding a Holy Mother in each arm, stood in the Piazza del Duomo and finally sold one to a huge German priest for twelve hundred; and the other she gave to a widow in weeds at Santa Maria Novella for eight hundred lire. F, when he heard, ground his teeth, and though she pleaded with him to be reasonable, swore he would carve no more.

He worked at odd jobs, one in a laundry, that tired him so he couldn't paint at night. One morning he tried chalking blue-robed Madonnas with Child, after Raphael, on the sidewalks before the Baptistery, Santa Chiara, the Stazione Centrale, where he was almost arrested. Passers-by stopped to watch him work but moved on quickly when he passed the hat. A few tossed small coins upon the image of the Holy Mother and F collected them and went to the next spot. A brown-robed monk in sandals followed him.

'Why don't you look for productive work?'

'Advice is cheap.'

'So is your art.'

He went to the Cappella Brancacci and sat the rest of the day staring in the half dark at the Masaccio frescoes. Geniuses made masterworks. If you weren't greatly gifted the way was hard, a masterwork was a miracle. Still, somehow or other art abounded in miracles.

He borrowed a fishing pole from an artist neighbour and fished, amid a line of men with bent rods, off the Ponte Trinita. F tied the rod to a nail on the railing and paced back and forth, returning every few minutes to check his line as the float bobbed in the Arno. He caught nothing, but the old fisherman next to him, who had pulled in eight fish, gave him a one-eyed crippled eel. It was a cloudy November day, then rainy, patches of damp appearing on the studio ceiling. The cornucopia leaked. The house was cold, Fabio wouldn't turn on the heat till December. It was hard to get warm. But Esmeralda made a tasty crippled-eel soup. The next night she cooked a handful of borrowed polenta that popped in the pot as it boiled. For lunch the following day there was stale bread and half an onion apiece.

But for Sunday supper she served boiled meat, green beans and a salad of beet leaves. He suspiciously asked how come, and she admitted she had borrowed a few hundred lire from Ludovico.

'How are we supposed to pay him back?'

'We won't, he owes me plenty.'

'Don't borrow from him any more.'

'I'm not afraid of him, he's afraid of me.'

'I don't like him coming around. I'm at my most dishonest among dishonest men.'

'Don't trust him, Arturo,' she said, frightened. 'He'd knife you if he could.'

'He won't get the chance.'

Afterwards she asked, 'Why don't you carve a Madonna or two? Two thousand lire now and then is nothing to spit at. Besides you do beautiful work in wood.'

'Not for the price, it's not worth my time.'

The landlord, wearing a woman's black shawl, entered without knocking, shouting for his rent.

'I'll get the municipality to throw you both out, the puttana and you. You're fouling up this house with your illicit activities. Your friend told me what goes on here. I have all the necessary information.'

'You know where you can stick it,' said F. 'If we weren't here the flat would go to ruin. It was empty six years before I moved in, you'll never rent it if I move out.'

'You're no Florentine,' Fabio shouted. 'You're not even an Italian.'

F got himself a badly paid job as journeyman in a woodworking establishment, not Panenero's. He worked long hours turning out delicate tapered legs for antique tables and did no painting. In the street, going back and forth from work, he looked for coins people might have dropped.

He switched off the light after Esmeralda had washed the supper dishes, watched carefully what she cooked, and ate, and doled out shopping money sparsely. Once she sold six inches of her hair to a man with a sack who had knocked on the door, so she could buy herself some warm underwear.

Finally she could stand it no longer. 'What are you going to do?'

'What can I do that I haven't?'

'I don't know. Do you want me to go back to my work?'

'I never said so.'

'If I don't you'll be like this for ever. It's what you're like when you're not painting.'

He remained mute.

'Why don't you speak?'

'What can I say?'

'You can say no.'

'No,' he said.

'It sounds like yes.'

He went out for a long walk and for a while hung around the palazzo where Dostoevsky had written the last pages of *The Idiot*. It did no good. When he returned he said nothing to Esmeralda. In fact he did not feel too bad though he knew he ought to. In fact he had been thinking of asking her to go to work, whatever she might do. It's circumstances, he thought.

Esmeralda had got out her black hat, the two dresses, and her gold shoes. On the velvet hat she sewed the silver roses. She raised the hems of the dresses above her knees and unstitched the necklines to expose the rounded tops of her hard breasts. The purple sequins she threw into the garbage.

'Anyway, I'll need protection,' she said.

'How do you mean?'

'You know what I mean. I don't want those bastards hurting me or not paying in full. It's blood money.'

'I'll protect you,' F said.

He wore dark glasses, a black velour hat pulled low over one eye and a brown overcoat with a ratty fur collar buttoned tight under the chin and extending to his ankles; he walked in white sneakers. He thought of growing a beard but gave that up. His bristly reddish moustache was thicker than it had ever been. And he carried a snappy cane with a slender sword inside.

They went together to the Piazza della Repubblica, almost merrily. 'For art,' she said, then after a moment, bitterly, 'art, my ass.'

She cursed him from the depth of her heart and then forgave him. 'It's my nature,' she said. 'I can't bear a grudge.'

He promised to marry her once he had finished the painting.

F paints all morning after Esmeralda has posed; she bathes, does her nails and toes and makes herself up with mascara. After a leisurely lunch they leave the house and go across the bridge to the Piazza della Repubblica. She sits on a bench with her legs crossed high, smoking; and F is at a bench near by, sketching in a pad in which he sometimes finds himself drawing dirty pictures: men and women, women and women, men and men. But he doesn't consort with the other pimps who sit together playing cards; nor does Esmeralda talk with the other whores, they call her hoity-toity. When a man approaches to ask whether she happens to be free she nods, or looking at him through her short veil, says yes as though she could just as well have said no. She gets up, the other whores watching her with their eyes and mouths, and wanders with her client into one of the crooked side streets, to a tiny room they have rented close by so there's no waste of man-hours getting back to the piazza. The room has a bed, water bowl, chamber pot.

When Esmeralda rises from the bench, F slips his drawing pad into his coat pocket and leisurely follows them. Sometimes it is a beautiful late-fall afternoon and he takes deep breaths as he walks. On occasion he stops to pick up a pack of Nazionale, and if he's a little hungry, gulps an espresso and a bit of pastry. He then goes up the smelly stairs and waits outside the door, sketching little pictures in the dim electric glow, as Esmeralda performs; or files his fingernails. It takes fifteen or twenty minutes for the customer to come out. Some would like to stay longer but can't if they won't pay for it. As a rule there are no arguments. The man dresses and sometimes leaves a tip if it has been most enjoyable. Esmeralda is still dressing, bored with getting in and out of her clothes. Only once thus far has she had to call F in to deal with a runt who said it hadn't been any good so no sense paying.

F enters with the sword drawn out of his cane and points it at the man's hairy throat. 'Pay,' he says, 'and beat it.' The runt, gone two shades white, hurriedly leaves assisted by a boot in the pants. Esmeralda watches without expression. She hands F the money – usually two thousand lire, sometimes three; and if she can get it from a wealthy-type client, or an older man especially fond of eighteen-year-old girls, seven or eight thousand. That sum is rare. F counts the money – often in small bills – and slips it into his wallet, wrapping a fat rubber band around it. In the evening they go home together, Esmeralda doing her shopping on the way. They try not to work at night unless it's been a bad day. In that case they go out after supper, when the piazza is lit in neon signs and the bars and cafés are doing business; the competition is stiff – some very beautiful women in extraordinary clothes. F goes into the bars and seeks out men who seem to be alone. He asks them if they want a pretty girl, and if one shows interest, leads him to Esmeralda. When it's rainy or freezing cold, they stay in and play cards or listen to the radio. F has opened an account in the Banco di Santo Spirito so they can draw from it in the winter if Esmeralda is sick and can't work. They go to bed after midnight. The next morning F gets up early and paints. Esmeralda sleeps late.

One morning F paints with his dark glasses on, until she wakes up and screams at him.

Later, when she is out buying material for a dress, Ludovico strides into the studio, incensed. His usually pallid face is flushed. He shakes his malacca at F.

'Why wasn't I informed that she had gone back to work? I demand a commission. She took all her instruction from me!'

F is about to run him out of the room by the worn seat of his overcoat but then has this interesting thought: Ludovico could take her over while he stays home to paint all day, for which he would pay him eight per cent of Esmeralda's earnings.

'Per cortesia,' says the pimp haughtily. 'At the very least twenty-five per cent. I have many obligations and am a sick man besides.'

'Eight is all we can afford, not a penny more.'

Esmeralda returns with a package or two and when she comprehends what the argument is, swears she will quit rather than work with Ludovico.

'You can do your own whoring,' she says to F. 'I'll go back to Fiesole.'

He tries to calm her. 'It's just that he's so sick is the reason I thought I'd cut him in.'

'Sick?'

'He's got one lung.'

'He has three lungs and four balls.'

F heaves the pimp down the stairs.

In the afternoon he sits on a bench not far from Esmeralda's in the Piazza della Repubblica, sketching himself on his drawing pad.

Esmeralda burned Bessie's old snapshot when F was in the toilet. 'I'm getting old,' she said, 'where's my future?' F considered strangling her but couldn't bring himself to; besides, he hadn't been using the photo since having Esmeralda as model. Still, for a time he felt lost without it, the physical presence of the decaying snap his only visible link to Ma, Bessie, the past. Anyway, now that it was gone it was gone, a memory become intangible again. He painted with more fervour yet detachment; fervour to complete the work, detachment towards image, object, subject. Esmeralda left him to his devices, went off for most of the afternoon and handed him the lire, fewer than before, when she returned. He painted with new confidence, amusement, wonder. The subject had changed from 'Mother and Son' to 'Brother and Sister' (Esmeralda as Bessie), to let's face it, 'Prostitute and Procurer'. Though she no longer posed, he was becoming clearer in his inner eye as to what he wanted. Once he retained her face for a week before scraping it off. I'm getting there. And though he considered sandpapering his own face off and substituting Ludovico as pimp, the magnificent thing was that in the end he kept himself in. This is my most honest piece of work. Esmeralda was the now nineteen-year-old prostitute; and he, with a stroke here and there ageing himself a bit, a fifteen-year-old procurer. This was the surprise that made the painting. And what it means, I suppose, is I am what I became from a young age. Then he thought, it has no meaning, a painting's a painting.

The picture completed itself. F was afraid to finish it: What would he do next and how long would that take? But the picture was, one day, done. It assumed a completion: This woman and man together, prostitute and procurer. She was a girl with fear in both black eyes, a vulnerable if stately neck, and a steely small mouth; he was a boy with tight insides, on the verge of crying. The presence of each protected the other. A Holy Sacrament. The form leaped to the eye. He had tormented, ecstatic, yet confused feelings, but at last felt triumphant – it was done! Though deeply drained, moved, he was satisfied, completed – ah, art!

He called Esmeralda to look at the painting. Her lips trembled, she lost colour, turned away, finally she spoke. 'For me it's me. You've caught me as I am, there's no doubt of it. The picture is a marvel.' She wept as she gazed at it. 'Now I can quit what I'm doing. Let's get married, Arturo.'

Ludovico, limping a little in his squeaky shoes, came upstairs to beg their pardons, but when he saw the finished painting on the easel stood stiff in awe.

'I'm speechless,' he said, 'what more can I say?'

'Don't bother,' said Esmeralda, 'nobody wants your stinking opinion.'

They opened a bottle of Soave and Esmeralda borrowed a pan and baked a loin of veal, to celebrate. Their artist neighbours came in, Citelli, an illustrator, and his dark meagre wife; it was a festive occasion. F afterwards related the story of his life and they all listened, absorbed.

When the neighbours left and the three were alone, Ludovico objectively discussed his weak nature.

'Compared to some I've met in the streets of Florence, I'm not a bad person, but my trouble is I forgive myself too easily. That has its disadvantages because then there are no true barriers to a harmful act, if you understand my meaning. It's the easy way out, but what else can you do if you grew up with certain disadvantages? My father was criminally inclined and it's from him I inherited my worst tendencies. It's clear enough that goats don't have puppies. I'm vain, selfish, although not arrogant, and given almost exclusively to petty evil. Nothing serious but serious enough. Of course I've wanted to change my ways, but at my age what can one change? Can you change yourself, maestro? Yet I readily confess who I am and ask your pardon for any inconvenience I might have caused you in the past. Either of you.'

'Drop dead,' said Esmeralda.

'The man's sincere,' F said, irritated. 'There's no need to be so cruel.'

'Come to bed, Arturo.' She entered the gabinetto as Ludovico went on with his confession.

'To tell the truth, I am myself a failed artist, but at least I contribute to the creativity of others by offering fruitful suggestions, though you're free to do as you please. Anyway, your painting is a marvel. Of course it's Picassoid, but you've outdone him in some of his strategies.'

F expressed thanks and gratitude.

'At first glance I thought that since the bodies of the two figures are so much more thickly painted than their faces, especially the girl's, this destroyed the unity of surface, but

125

when I think of some of the impastos I've seen, and the more I study your painting, the more I feel that's not important.'

'I don't think it'll bother anybody so long as it looks like a spontaneous act.'

'True, and therefore my only criticism is that maybe the painting suffers from an excess of darkness. It needs more light. I'd say a soupçon of lemon and a little red, not more than a trace. But I leave it to you.'

Esmeralda came out of the gabinetto in a red nightgown with a black lace bodice.

'Don't touch it,' she warned. 'You'll never make it better.'

'How would you know?' F said.

'I have my eyes.'

'Maybe she's right,' Ludovico said, with a yawn. 'Who knows with art? Well, I'm on my way. If you want to sell your painting for a handsome price, my advice is take it to a reliable dealer. There are one or two in the city whose names and addresses I'll bring you in the morning.'

'Don't bother,' Esmeralda said. 'We don't need your assistance.'

'I want to keep it around for a few days to look at,' F confessed.

'As you please.' Ludovico tipped his hat good night and left limping. F and Esmeralda went to bed together. Later she returned to her cot in the kitchen, took off her red nightgown and put on an old one of white muslin.

F for a while wondered what to paint next. Maybe sort of a portrait of Ludovico, his face reflected in a mirror, with two sets of aqueous sneaky eyes. He slept soundly but in the middle of the night awoke depressed. He went over his painting inch by inch and it seemed to him a disappointment. Where was Momma after all these years? He got up to look, and doing so, changed his mind; not bad at all, though Ludovico was right, the picture was dark and could stand a touch of light. He laid out his paints and brushes and began to work, almost at once achieving the effect he sought. And then he thought he would work a bit on the girl's face, no more than a stroke or two around the eyes and mouth, to make her expression truer to life. More the prostitute, himself a little older. When the sun blazed through both windows, he realized he had been working for hours. F put down his brush, washed up and returned for a look at the painting. Sickened to his gut, he saw what he felt: He had ruined it. It slowly drowned in his eyes.

Ludovico came in with a well-dressed paunchy friend, an art dealer. They looked at the picture and laughed.

Five long years down the drain. F squeezed a tube of black on the canvas and with a thick brush smeared it over both faces in all directions.

When Esmeralda pulled open the curtain and saw the mess, moaning, she came at him with the bread knife. 'Murderer!'

F twisted it out of her grasp, and in anguish lifted the blade into his gut.

'This serves me right.'

'A moral act,' Ludovico agreed.

5

Fidelman pissing in muddy water discovers water over his head. Modigliani wanders by searching by searchlight for his lost statues in Livorno canal. They told me to dump them in the canal, so I fucked them, I dumped them. Ne ha viste? Macchè. How come that light works underwater? Hashish. If we wake we drown, says Fidelman. *Chants de Maldoror.* His eyeless face drained of blood but not yellow light, Modi goes up canal as Fidelman drifts down.

Woodcut. Knight, Death and the Devil. Dürer.

Au fond il s'est suicidé. Anon.

Broken rusting balls of Venus. Ah, to sculpt a perfect hole, the volume and gravity constant. Invent space. Surround matter with hole rather than vice versa. That would have won me enduring fame and fortune and spared me all this wandering.

Cathedral of Erotic Misery. Schwitters.

Everybody says you're dead, otherwise why do you never write? Madonna Adoring the Child, Mater Dolorosa. Madonna della Peste. Long White Knights. Lives of the Saints. S. Sebastian, arrow collector, swimming in bloody sewer. Pictured transfixed with arrows. S. Denis, decapitated. Pictured holding his head. S. Agatha, breasts shorn clean, running enflamed. Painted carrying both bloody breasts in white salver. S. Stephen, crowned with rocks. Shown stoned. S. Lucy tearing out eyes for suitor smitten by same. Portrayed bearing two-eyed omelette on dish. S. Catherine, broken apart on spiked wheel. Pictured married to wheel. S. Laurence, roasted on slow grill. *I am roasted on one side. Now turn me over and eat.* Shown cooked but uneaten. S. Bartholomew, flayed alive. Standing with skin draped over skinned arm. S. Fima, eaten by rats. Pictured with happy young rat. S. Simon Zelotes, sawed in half. Shown with bleeding crosscut saw. S. Genet in prison, pictured with boys. S. Fidel Uomo, stuffing his ass with flowers.

Still Life with Herrings. S. Soutine.

He divideth the gefilte fish and matzos.

Drawing. Flights of birds over dark woods, sparrows, finches, thrushes, white doves, martins, swallows, eagles. Birds with human faces crapping human on whom they crap.

Wood sculpture. Man holding sacrificial goat. Cubist goat with triangular titties. Goat eating hanged goat.

The Enigma of Isidor Ducasse. Man Ray.

In this time Fidelman, after making studies of the work of Donatello, in particular of the Annunciation carved in stone for the church of S. Croce, the S. George in armour, with all the beauty of youth and the courage of the knight, and the bald man known as Il Zuccone, from figures in the façade of Giotto's Campanile, about whom it was said the sculptor, addressing his creation, would cry out, Speak, Speak: In this time the American began to work in original images dug into the soil. To those who expressed astonishment regarding this extraordinary venture, Fidelman is said to have replied, Being a poor man I can neither purchase nor borrow hard or soft stone; therefore, since this is so, I create my figures as hollows in the earth. In sum, my material is the soil, my tools a pickaxe and shovel, my sculpture the act of digging rather than carving or assembling. However, the pleasure in creation is not less than that felt by Michelangelo.

After attempting first several huge ziggurats that because of the rains tumbled down like Towers of Babel, he began to work labyrinths and mazes dug in the earth and constructed in the form of jewels. Later he refined and simplified this method, building a succession of spontaneously placed holes, each a perfect square, which when seen together constituted a sculpture. These Fidelman exhibited throughout Italy in whatsoever place he came.

Having arrived in a city carrying his tools on his shoulder and a few possessions in a knotted bundle on his arm, the sculptor searched in the environs until he had come upon a small plot of land he could dig on without the formality of paying rent. Because this good fortune was not always possible, he was more than once rudely separated from his sculptures as they were in the act of being constructed, and by the tip of someone's boot, ejected from the property whereon he worked, the hollows then being filled in by the angry landowners. For this reason the sculptor often chose public places and dug in parks, or squares, if this were possible, which to do so he sometimes pretended, when questioned by officials of the police, that he was an underground repairman sent there by the Municipality. If he was disbelieved by these and dragged off to jail, he lay several days recuperating from the efforts of his labours, not unpleasantly. There are worse places than jails, Fidelman is said to have said, and once I am set free I shall begin my sculptures in another place. To sum up, he dug where he could, yet not far from the marketplace where many of the inhabitants of the city passed by daily, and where, if he was not unlucky, the soil was friable and not too hard with rock to be dug. This task he performed, as was his custom, quickly and expertly. Just as Giotto is said to have been able to draw a perfect free-hand circle, so could Fidelman dig a perfect square hole without measurement. He arranged the sculptures singly or in pairs according to the necessity of the Art. These were about a braccio in volume, sometimes two, or two-and-a-half if Fidelman was not too fatigued. The smaller sculpture took from two to three hours to construct, the larger perhaps five or six; and if the final grouping was to contain three pieces, this meant a long day, indeed, and possibly two, of continual digging. There were times when because of weariness Fidelman would have compromised for a single braccio piece; but in the end Art prevailed and he dug as he must to fulfil those forms that must be fulfilled.

After constructing his sculptures the artist, unwinding a canvas sign on stilts, advertised the exhibition. The admission requested was ten lire, which was paid to him in the roped-off entrance way, the artist standing with a container in his hand. Not many were enticed to visit the exhibition, especially when it snowed or rained, although Fidelman was heard to say that the weather did not the least harm to his sculptures, indeed, sometimes improved them by changing volume and texture as well as affecting other qualities. And it was as though nature, which until now was acted upon by the artist, now acted upon the Art itself, an unexpected but satisfying happening, since thus were changed the forms of a form. Even on the most crowded days when more than several persons came to view his holes in the earth, the sculptor earned a meagre sum, not more than two or three hundred lire at most. He well understood that his bread derived from the curious among the inhabitants,

rather than from the true lovers of Art, but for this pheno-
menon took no responsibility since it was his need to create
and not be concerned with the commerce of Art. Those few
who came to the exhibit, they viewed the sculptures at times
in amazement and disbelief, whether at the perfect constructions or at their own stupidity, if indeed they believed
they were stupid, is not known. Some of the viewers, after
gazing steadfastly at the sculptures, were like sheep in their
expression, as if wondering whether they had been deceived;
some were stony faced, as if they knew they had been. But
few complained aloud, being ashamed to admit their folly,
if indeed it were folly. To the one or two who rudely questioned him, saying, Why do you pass off on us as sculpture
an empty hole or two? the artist, with the greatest tact and
courtesy, replied, It were well if you relaxed before my
sculptures, if you mean to enjoy them, and yield yourself
to the pleasure they evoke in the surprise of their forms.
At these words he who had complained fell silent, not
certain he had truly understood the significance of the
work of Art he had seen. On occasion a visitor would
speak to the artist to compliment him, which he received
with gratitude. Eh, maestro, your sculptures touch my heart.
I thank you from the bottom of my own, the artist is said to
have replied, blowing his nose to hide the gratification that
he felt.

There is a story told that in Naples in a small park near
the broad avenue called Via Carracciola, one day a young
man waited until the remaining other visitor had left the
exhibit so that he might speak to the sculptor. Maestro,
said he most earnestly, it distresses me to do so, but I must
pray you to return to me the ten lire I paid for admission
to your exhibit. I have seen no more than two square holes
in the ground and am much dissatisfied. The fault lies

in you that you have seen only holes, Fidelman is said to have replied. I cannot, however, return the admission fee to you, for doing so might cause me to lose confidence in my work. Why do you refuse me my just request? said the poorly attired young man, whose dark eyes, although intense and comely, were mournful. I ask for my young babes. My wife gave me money so that I might buy bread for our supper, of which we have little. We are poor folk and I have no steady work. Yet when I observed the sign calling attention to your sculptures, which though I looked for them I could see none visible, I was moved by curiosity, an enduring weakness of mine and the cause of much of my misery. It came into my heart that I must see these sculptures, so I gave up the ten lire, I will confess, in fear and trepidation, hoping to be edified and benefited although fearful I would not be. I hoped that your sculptures, since they are described on the banner as new in the history of Art, might teach me what I myself must make in order that I may fulfil my desire to be great in Art; but all I can see are two large holes, the one dug deeper by about a braccio than the other. Holes are of no use to me, my life being full of them, so I beg you to return the lire that I may hasten to the baker's shop to buy the bread I was sent for.

After hearing him out, Fidelman is said to have answered, I do not as a rule explain my sculptures to the public, but since you are an attractive young man who has turned his thoughts to becoming an artist, I will say to you what your eyes have not seen, in order that you may be edified and benefited.

I hope that may be so, said the young man, although I doubt it.

Listen before you doubt. Primus, although the sculpture is more or less invisible it is sculpture nevertheless. Because you can't see it doesn't mean it isn't there. As for use or uselessness, rather think that that is Art which is made by the artist to be Art. Secundus, you must keep in mind that any sculpture is a form existing at a point radiating in all directions, therefore since it is dug into the Italian earth the sculpture vibrates overtones of Italy's Art, history, politics, religion; even nature as one experiences it in this country. There is also a metaphysic in relation of down to up, and vice versa, but I won't pursue that matter now. Suffice to say, my sculpture is not unrelated, though not necessarily purposefully, to its environment, whether seen or unseen. Tertius, in relation to the above, it is impossible to describe the range of choices, conscious or unconscious, that exist in the creation of a single sculptured hole. However, let it be understood that choice, as I use the word in this context, means artistic freedom, for I do not in advance choose the exact form and position of the hole; it chooses me. The essential thing is to maintain contact with it as it is being achieved. If the artist loses contact with his hole, than which there is none like it in the universe; then the hole will not respond and the sculpture will fail. Thus I mean to show you that constructs of a sculpture which appear to be merely holes are, in truth, in the hands of the artist, elements of a conceptual work of Art.

You speak well, maestro, but I am dull-witted and find it difficult to comprehend such things. It would not surprise me that I forgot what you have so courteously explained before I arrive at the next piazza. May I not therefore have the ten lire back? I will be ever grateful to you.

Tough titty if you can't comprehend Art, Fidelman is said to have replied. Fuck off now.

The youth left, sighing, without his ten lire, nor with bread for his babes.

Not long after he had departed, as it grew dusk, the sculptor took down the banner of his exhibit and gathered his tools so that he might fill in the sculpture and leave for another city. As he was making these preparations a stranger appeared, wrapped in the folds of a heavy cloak, although winter still hid in its cave and the fields were ripe with grain. The stranger's nether limbs, clothed in coarse black stockings, were short and bowed, and his half-concealed visage, iron eyes in a leather face, caused the flesh on Fidelman's neck to prickle and thicken. But the stranger, averting his glance and speaking pleasantly, yet as though to his own hands, and in the accent of one from a foreign land, graciously prayed the sculptor for permission to view his sculpture, the effect of which he had heard was extraordinary. He explained he had been delayed on board ship and apologized for appearing so late in the day. Fidelman, having recovered somewhat from his surprise at the stranger's odd garments and countenance, is said to have replied it made no difference that he had come late so long as he paid the admission fee.

This the stranger did forthwith with a gold coin for which he neither asked nor received change. He glanced fleetingly at the sculpture and turned away as though dazzled, the which the sculptor is said to have wondered at.

But instead of departing the exhibit now that he had viewed it, however hastily, the stranger tarried, his back to that place where the sculpture stood fixed in the earth, the red sun sinking at his shoulders. As though reflecting still upon that he had seen, he consumed an apple, the core of which he tossed over his left shoulder into one of the holes of the sculpture; an act that is said to have angered Fidelman although he refrained from complaint, it may be because he feared this stranger was an agent of the police, so it were better he said nothing.

If you'll excuse me, said the stranger at last, please explain to me what means these two holes that they have in them nothing but the dark inside?

The meaning lies in what they are as they seem to be, and the dark you note within, although I did not plan it so or put it there, may be thought of as an attribute of the aesthetic, Fidelman is said to have replied.

So what then did you put there?

To wit, the sculpture.

At that the stranger laughed, his laughter not unlike the bray of a goat. All I saw was nothing. To me, if you'll pardon me, is a hole nothing. This I will prove to you. If you will look in the small hole there is now there an apple core. If not for this would be empty the hole. If empty would be there nothing.

Emptiness is not nothing if it has form.

Form, if you will excuse me my expression, is not what is the whole of Art.

One might argue that, but neither is content if that's what you intend to imply. Form may be and often is the content of Art.

You don't say?

I do indeed.

The stranger spat on both of his hands and rubbed them together, a disagreeable odour rising from them.

In this case I will give you form.

Since the stranger stood now scarce visible in the dark, the sculptor began to be in great fear, his legs, in truth, trembling.

Who are you? Fidelman is said finally to have demanded.

I am also that youth that he is now dead in the Bay of Naples, that you would not give him back his poor ten lire so he could buy bread for his babies.

Are you not the devil? the sculptor is said to have cried out.

I am also him.

Quid ego feci?

This I will tell you. You have not yet learned what is the difference between something and nothing.

Bending for the shovel, the stranger smote the horrified Fidelman with its blade a resounding blow on the head, the sculptor toppling as though dead into the larger of the two holes he himself had dug. He-who-Fidelman-did-not-know then proceeded to shovel in earth until the sculpture and its creator were extinguished.

So it's a grave, the stranger is said to have muttered. So now we got form but we also got content.

Collage. The Flayed Ox. Rembrandt. Hanging Fowl. Soutine. Young Man with Death's Head. Van Leyden. Funeral at Ornans. Courbet. Bishop Eaten by Worms. Murillo. Last Supper, Last Judgment, Last Inning.

I paint with my prick. Renoir. I paint with my ulcer. Soutine. I paint with my paint. Fidelman.

One can study nature, dissect and analyse and balance it without making paintings. Bonnard.

Gouache. Unemployed Musician. Fiddleman.

Painting is nothing more than the art of expressing the invisible through the visible. Fromentin. Indefinite Divisibility. Tanguy. Definite Invisibility. Fidelman.

I'm making the last paintings which anyone can make. Reinhardt. I've made them. I like my paintings because anyone can do them. Warhol. Me too.

Erased de Kooning Drawing. Rauschenberg. Erased

Rauschenberg de Kooning. Lithograph. Eraser. Fidelman.

Modigliani climbs and falls. He tries to scale a brick wall with bleeding fingers, his eyes lit crystals of heroin, whisky, pain. He climbs and falls in silence.

My God, what's all that climbing and falling for?

For art, you cretin.

Thunder and lightning.

Portrait of an Old Jew Seated. Rembrandt. Portrait of an Old Jew in an Armchair. Rembrandt. It beats walking.

Then I dreamt that I woke suddenly, with an unspeakable shock, to the consciousness that someone was lying in bed beside me. I put my hand out and touched the soft naked shoulder of a woman; and a cold gentle little woman's voice said: I have not been in bed for a hundred years. Raverat. The Rat Killer. Rembrandt.

Elle m'a mordu aux couilles. Modigliani.

Mosaic. Piazza Amerina, Sicily. IVth Cent. A.D. All that remains after so long a time.

Susskind preacheth up on the mountain, a piece of green palm branch behind his head. (He has no halo, here the mosaic is broken.) Three small cactus plants groweth at his bare feet./ Tell the truth. Dont cheat. If its easy it dont mean its good. Be kind, specially to those that they got less than you. I want for everybody justice. Must also be charity. If you feel good give charity. If you feel bad give charity. Must also be mercy. Be nice, dont fight. Children, how can we live without mercy? If you have no mercy for me I shall not live. Love, mercy, charity. Its not so easy believe me.

At the bottom of the brown hill they stand there by the huge lichenous rock that riseth above them on the top of which is a broad tree with a twisted trunk./ Ah, Master, my eyes watereth. Thou speakest true. I love thy words. I love thee more than thy words. If I could paint thee with my paints, then would my heart soar to the Gates of Heaven. I will be forever thy disciple, no ifs and buts./ This is already iffed. If you will follow me, follow. If you will follow must be for Who I Am. Also please, no paints or paintings. Remember the Law, what it says. No graven images, which is profanation and idolatry. Nobody can paint Who I Am. Not on papyrus, or make me into an idol of wood, or stone, not even in the sand. Dont try, its a sin. Here is a parable: And the Lord called unto Moses and spoke to him, Moses, come thou on this mountain and I will show Myself so thou mayst see Me, and none but thee; and Moses answered: Lord, if I see Thee, then wilt Thou become as a graven image on mine eye and I be blind. Then spake the Lord, saying, Thou art my beloved Son, in whom I am well pleased, and for this there is no Promised Land./ Whats the parable of that? Its more a paradox, Id say./ If you dont know its not for you./ Tell me, Master, art thou the Living God? Art thou at least the Son of God?/ So we will see, its not impossible./ Art thou the Redeemer?/ This could be also, Im not sure myself. Depends what happens./ Is thy fate ordained?/ I act like I Am. Who knows my fate? All I know is somebody will betray me. Dont ask how I know, I know. You dont but I do. This is the difference./ It is not I, Master, I will never betray thee. Cast me out now if thou believest I speak not the TRUTH./ What happens will happen. So give up your paints and your brushes and follow me where I go, and we will see what we will see. This we will see./ Master, tis as good as done.

Fidelman droppeth into the Dead Sea all his paints and

139

brushes, except one. These dissolve in the salted sea. (A piece of the blue sea is faded.)

(In this picture) As Susskind preacheth to the multitude, on the shore of the green sea of Galilee where sail the little ships of the fisher men, as even the red fishes and the white fishes come to listen at the marge of the water, the black goats stand still on the hills, the painter, who hideth behind a palm tree, sketcheth with a coal on papyrus the face and figure of the Master./ If I could do a portrait of him as he is in this life I will be remembered forever in human history. Nobody can call that betrayal, I dont think, for its for the good of us all./ My child, why do you do that which I forbade you? Dont think I cant see you, I can. I wish I couldnt see what I see, but I can.

The painter kneeleth on his knees. (A few tesserae are missing from his face, including one of the eye, and a few black stones from his beard.)/ Master, forgive me. All I meant to do was preserve thy likeness for a future time. I guess it gotteth to be too much for me, the thought that I might. Forgive, forgive in thy mercy. Ill burn everything, I promise, papyrus, charcoal, a roll of canvas I have hid in my hut, also this last paint brush although a favourite of mine./ Listen to me, there are two horses, one brown, the other black. The brown obeys his master, the black does not. Which is the better horse?/ Both are the same./ How is this so?/ One obeys and the other does not, but they are both thoroughbreds./ You have an easy tongue. If I cant change you I must suffer my fate. This is a fact./ Master, have no further worries on that score, I am a changed man down to my toe nails, I give thee my word.

*　　*　　*　　*　　*

Fidelman speaketh to himself in a solitary place in Capernaum./ This talent it is death to hide lodged in me useless. How am I ever going to make a living or win my spurs? How can I compete in this world if both my hands are tied and my eyes blindfolded? Whats so moral about that? How is a man meant to fulfil himself if he isnt allowed to paint? Its graven image versus grave damages to myself and talent. Which harms the most there is no doubt. One can take just so much./ He gnasheth his teeth. He waileth to the sky. He teareth his cheeks and pulleth out the hairs of his head and beard. He butteth his skull against the crumbling brick wall. On this spot the wall is stained red with blood./ Satan saith Ha Ha.

As Susskind sat at meat he spoke thus. Verily I say, one of you who eats now at this table will betray me, dont ask who./ His followers blusheth. Their faces are in shades of pink. No one blusheth not. Fidelman blusheth red./ But if he knows, it cant be all that wrong to do it. What I mean is Im not doing it in any sneaky way, that is, for after all he knows./ He that has betrayed me once will betray me twice. He will betray me thrice./ Fidelman counteth on his fingers.

He is now in the abode of the high priest Caiaphas./ (Here the mosaic is almost all destroyed. Only the painter's short-fingered hand survives.) Fidelmans heavy hand is filled with thirty-nine pieces of silver.

The painter runneth out to buy paints, brushes, canvas.

On the Mount of Olives appeareth the painter amid a multitude with swords, staves, and lengths of lead pipe. Also come

the chief priest, the chief of police, scribes, elders, the guards
with dogs, the onlookers to look on. Fidelman goeth to the
master and kisseth him full on the lips./ Twice, saith Susskind./ He wept.

He hath on his head a crown of rusty chain links. A guard
smiteth his head and spitteth on his eye. In mockery they
worship Susskind./ Its a hard life, he saith./ He draggeth the
beam of the cross up a hill. Fidelman watcheth from behind
a mask.

12 12 12 12 12 12 12 12 12 12 12 12 12 12 12 12 12 12 12 12
369 369 369 369 369 369 369 369 369 369 369 369 369 369
veyizmirveyizmirveyizmirveyizmirveyizmirveyizmirveyizmi
12369123691236912369123691236912369123691236912369

Fidelman painteth three canvasses. The Crucifixion he
painteth red on red. The Descent from the Cross he painteth
white on white. For the Resurrection, on Easter morning, he
leaveth the canvas blank.

P

t o tem

L

E

Suss

King

Je vous emmerde. Modigliani.

Oil on wood. Bottle fucking guitar? Bull impaled on pole?
One-eyed carp stuffed in staring green bottle? Clown
spooning dog dung out of sawdust? Staircase ascending a
nude? Black-stockinged whore reading pornographic book

142

by lamplight? Still life: three apple cores plus one long grey hair? Boy pissing on old man's shoe? The blue disease? Balding woman dyeing her hair? Buggers of Calais? Blood oozing from ceiling on foggy night?

Rembrandt was the first great master whose sitters sometimes dreaded seeing their portraits. Malraux. I is another. Rimbaud.

1. Watercolour. Tree growing in all directions. Nothing nameable taxonomically speaking, like weeping willow with stiff spotted leaves, some rotted brown-green. Otherwise stylized apple-green-to-gold leaves. Not maple or sycamore same though resembling both, enlarged, painted to cover whole tree from roots to topmost spotted leaf. The leaves are the tree. Branches like black veins, thins to thicks, visible behind or through leaves. No birds in tree, not rook or raven. Impression is of mystery. Nothing more is seen at first but if viewer keeps looking tree is cleverly a human face. Leaves and branches delineate strained features, also lonely hollow anguished eyes. What is this horror I am or represent? Painter can think of none, for portrait is of a child and he remembers happy childhood, or so it seems. Exactly what face has done, or where has been, or knows, or wants to know, or is or isn't experiencing, isn't visible, nor can be explained as tone, memory, feeling; or something that happened in later life that painter can't recall. Maybe it never happened. It's as though this face is hiding in a tree or pretending to be one while waiting for something to happen in life and that something when it happened was nothing. Nothing much. 2. Triptych. Woodcut. It's about forbidden love. In the first black-and-white panel this guy is taking his sister in her black-and-white bathrobe. She squirms but loves it. Can be done in white-and-black for contrast. Man Seducing Sister or Vice Versa. The second

panel is about the shame of the first, where he takes to masturbating in the cellar. It's dark so you can't see much of his face but there's just enough light to see what he's up to. Man Spilling Seed on Damp Cellar Floor. Then here in this third panel, two men doing it, each with his three-fingered hand on the other's maulstick. This can be inked darkly because they wouldn't want to be seen. 3. Then having prepared it for painting he began to think what he would paint upon it that would frighten everyone that saw it, having the effect of the head of Medusa. So he brought for that purpose to his room, which no one entered but himself, lizards, grasshoppers, serpents, butterflies, locusts, bats, and other strange animals of the kind, and from them all he produced a great animal so horrible and fearful that it seemed to poison the air with its fiery breath. This he represented coming out of some dark rocks with venom issuing from its open jaws, fire from its eyes, and smoke from its nostrils, a monstrous and horrible thing indeed. Lives of the Painters: Leonardo. 4. Figure; wood, string, and found objects. Picasso.

Incisore. The cylinder, the sphere, the cone. Cézanne. The impact of an acute angle of a triangle on a circle promises an effect no less powerful than the finger of God touching the finger of Adam in Michelangelo, Kandinsky.

Fidelman, etcher, left a single engraving of the series called A Painter's Progress. Originally there were six copper plates, drypoint, all with their prints destroyed, how or why is not known. Only a single imperfect artist's proof entitled 'The Cave' survives. This etching represents a painter at work, resemblance to whom may easily be guessed. Each night, according to a tattered diary he had kept for a while, he entered the cave in question through a cellar he had the key to, when all the lights in the old clapboard house, several boards missing, were out, curtains thickly drawn over each narrow window. The painter in the etching worked all night, night after night, inch by slow inch covering the rough limestone surface of the voluminous cave at the end of a labyrinth under the cellar, with intricate designs of geometric figures; and he left before dawn, his coming and going unknown to his sister, who lived in the house alone. The walls and part of the roof of the huge cave that he had been decorating for years and years and estimated at least two more to go before his labours were ended, were painted in an extraordinary tapestry of simple figures in black, salmon, gold-yellow, sea-green and apricot, although the colours cannot of course be discerned in the three-toned engraving – a rich design of circles and triangles, discrete or interlocking, of salmon triangles encompassed within apricot circles, and sea-green circles within pale gold-yellow triangles, blown like masses of autumn leaves over the firmament of the cave.

The painter of the cave, wearing a leafy loincloth as he laboured, varied the patterns of the geometric design. He was at that time of his life engaged in developing a more intricate conception of circles within circles of various hues and shades including copper red and light olive; and to extend his art further, of triangles within triangles within concentric circles. He drove himself at his work, intending when his labour was done to climb the dark stairs ascending to his sister's first floor and tell her what he had accomplished in the cave below. Bessie, long a widow, all her children married and scattered across the continent, her oldest daughter in Montreal, lived, except for occasional visitors, mostly the doctor, alone in the old frame house she had come to as a young bride, in Newark, New Jersey. She was at this time, ill and possibly dying. Nobody he could think of had told her artist-brother, but he figured he somehow knew. Call it intuition. It was his hope she would remain alive until he had completed his art work of the cave and she could at last see how it had turned out.

Bessie, he would say, I did this for you and you know why.

Fidelman worked by the light of a single dusty 100-watt bulb, the old-fashioned kind with a glass spicule at the bottom, dangling from a wire from the ceiling of the cave, that he had installed when he first came there to paint. For a long time he had distrusted the bulb because he had never had to replace it, and sometimes it glowed like a waning moon after he had switched it off, making him feel slightly uneasy and a little lumpy in the chest. He suspected a presence, immanent or otherwise, around; though who or why, and under what circumstances, he could not say. Nothing or nobody substantial. Anyway, he didn't care for the bulb. He knew why when it began, one night, to speak to him. How does a bulb speak? With the sound of light. Fidelman for a while did not respond, first because he couldn't, his throat constricted; and second, because he suspected this might be he talking to himself; yet when it spoke again, this time he answered.

Fidelman, said the voice of, or from within, the bulb, why are you here such a long time in this cave? Painting – this we know – but why do you paint so long a whole cave? What kind of business is this?

Leaving my mark is what. For the ages to see. This place will someday be crowded with visitors at a dollar a throw. Mark my words.

But why in this way if there are better?

What would you suggest, for instance?

Whatever I suggest is too late now, but why don't you

go at least upstairs and say hello to your sister who hasn't seen you in years? Go before it is too late, because she is now dying.

Not quite just yet I can't go, said the painter. I can't until my work is finished because I want to show her what I've accomplished once it's done.

Go up to her now, this is the last chance. Your work in this cave will take years yet. Tell her at least hello. What have you got to lose? To her it will be a wonderful thing.

No, I can't. It's all too complicated. I can't go till I've finished the job. The truth is I hate the past. It caught me unawares. I'd rather not see her just yet. Maybe next week or so.

It's a short trip up the stairs to say hello to her. What can you lose if it's only fourteen steps and then you're there?

It's too complicated, like I said. I hate the past.

So why do you blame her for this?

I don't blame anybody at all. I just don't want to see her. At least not just yet.

If she dies she's dead. You can talk all you want then but she won't answer you.

It's no fault of mine if people die. There's nothing I can do about it.

Nobody is talking about fault or not fault. All we are talking about is to go upstairs.

I can't I told you, it's too complicated, I hate the past, it caught me unawares. If there's anything to blame I don't blame her. I just don't want to see her is all, at least not just yet until my work here is done.

Don't be so proud my friend. Pride ain't spinach. You can't eat it, so it won't make you grow. Remember what happened to the Greeks.

Praxiteles? He who first showed Aphrodite naked? Phidias, whose centaur's head is thought to be a self-portrait? Who have you got in mind?

No, the one that he tore out his eyes. Watch out for hubris. It's poison ivy. Trouble you got enough, you want also blisters? Also an electric bulb don't give so often advice so listen with care. When did you hear last that an electric bulb gave advice? Did I advise Napoleon? Did I advise Van Gogh? This is like a miracle, so why don't you take advantage and go upstairs?

Well, you've got a point there. There's some truth to it, I suppose. I might at that, come to think of it. As you say, it's not everybody who gets advice in this way. There's something Biblical about it, if I may say. Furthermore, I'm not getting any younger and I haven't seen Bessie in years. Plus I do owe her something, after all. Be my Virgil, which way to up the stairs?

I will show you which way but I can't go with you. Up to a point but not further if you know what I mean. A bulb is a bulb. Light I got but not feet. After all, this is the Universe, everything is laws.

Fidelman slowly climbs up the stone, then wooden, stairs, lit generously from bottom clear to top by the bulb, and opens the creaking door into a narrow corridor. He walks along it till he comes to a small room where Bessie is lying in a sagging double bed.

Hello, Bessie, I've been downstairs most of the time, but I came up to say hello.

Why are you so naked, Arthur? It's winter outside.

It's how I am nowadays.

Arthur, said Bessie, why did you stop writing for so long? Why didn't you answer my letters?

I guess I had nothing much to write. Nothing much has happened to me. There wasn't much to say.

Remember how Mama used to give us an apple to eat with a slice of bread?

I don't like to remember those things any more.

Anyway, thanks for coming up to see me, Arthur. It's a nice thing to do when a person is so alone. At least I know what you look like and where you are nowadays.

Bessie died and rose to heaven, holding in her heart her brother's hello.

Flights of circles, cones, triangles.

End of drypoint etching.

The ugly and plebeian face with which Rembrandt was ill-favoured was accompanied by untidy and dirty clothes, since it was his custom, when working, to wipe his brushes on himself, and to do other things of a similar nature. Jakob Rosenberg.

If you're dead how do you go on living?

Natura morta: still life. Oil on paper.

6

Venice, floating city of green and golden canals. Fidelman floated too, from stem to stern. When the sirocco relentlessly blew in late autumn the island dipped on ancient creaking piles towards the outer isles, then gently tipped to the mainland against the backwash of oily waters. The ex-painter, often seasick in the municipal garbage boat, fished with a net out of the smelly canals, dead rats and lettuce leaves. He had come for the Biennale and stayed on.

November fog settled on the webbed-canalled and narrow-streeted city, obscuring campanile, church steeples, and the red-tiled roofs of houses tilted together from opposite sides of streets. Oars splashing, he skirted the mist-moving vaporetti, his shouts and curses opposing their horns and the tolling bellbuoys in the lagoon. For Fidelman no buoy bells tolled, no church bells either; he kept no track of tide or time. On All Souls' Day, unable to resist, he rowed after a black-and-silver funeral barge and cortège of draped mourning gondolas moving like silent arrows across the water to San Michele, gloomy cypressed isle of the dead; the corpse of a young girl in white laid stiff in a casket covered with wreaths of hothouse flowers guarded by wooden angels. She waits, whatever she waited for, or sought, or hungered for, no longer. Ah, i poveri morti, though that depends on how you look at it. He had looked too long.

Fidelman, December ferryman, ferried standing passengers, their heads in mist, to the opposite rainy shore of the Grand Canal. Whichever shore. The wet winter rain drummed on the crooked roofs of the façade-eroded palazzi standing in undulating slime-green algae; and upon moving clusters of black bobbing umbrellas in the dark streets and marketplaces. The ex-painter wandered wet-hatted, seeking in shop windows who knows what treat the tourists hadn't coveted and bought. Venice was full of goods he hungered for and detested. Yet he sought an object of art nobody would recognize but Fidelman.

In January the cold swollen tides of the Adriatic rose again over the Mole, swirling a metre deep on the Piazza and flooding the pavimento of San Marco. If you had to, you could swim to the altar. Gondolas stealthily glided over the Stones of Venice, wet Bride of the Sea, drowning greenly an inch or two annually as Fidelman, a cold fish in his thin trousers, inch by inch also drowned, envisioning Tintoretto: 'Venice Overwhelmed by Tidal Wave.'

The rain blew away before the sunlit cold but not the pools and ponds, more than one campo alongside open water or canal, flooded. Fidelman staked a claim, having been fired from cross-canal transportation on the complaint of two patriotic gondoliers, and now did his ferrying piggyback for one hundred lire per person, skinny old men half-price if they didn't grip him too tightly around the neck. He had once read of a fiendish beggar who had strangled and drowned a good samaritan carrying him across a flooded brook. Fat people he served last, after he had ferried across the others on line, though they roundly berated him for prejudice, or offered twice the going rate. One aristocratic huge old dame with a voice that rose out of a tuba belaboured him with her slender silk umbrella.

Fidelman waded in hip boots through high water glinting like shards of broken mirror in the freezing winter sunlight, and deposited his customers on dry ground whence they proceeded hurriedly along narrow streets and alleys. Occasionally while transporting a female he gave her a modified feel along the leg, which roused no response through winter clothing; still it was good for the morale. One attractive, long-nosed, almost oriental-eyed young Venetian woman who mounted his back, began at once to giggle, and laughed, unable to control it, mirthfully as he slowly sloshed across the pond. She sat on Fidelman, enjoying the ride, her rump bumping his, cheek pressed to his frozen ear, hugging him casually, a pair of shapely black-stocking legs clasped in the crooks of his arms; and when he tenderly set her down, his penis erect, athrob, she kissed him affectionately and hastily went her way. As Fidelman watched she turned back, smiling sadly, as though they had once been lovers and the affair was ended. Then she waved good-bye and walked on. He wished she hadn't, for he was after a while in love with her.

When the water receded as the bora roared, drying the city, uncovering here and there a drowned cat, the winter light sprang up crystal clear as Fidelman, once more jobless, holding on to his hat – you can't chase them on the canals – sought his lady, to no avail. He searched from the Public Gardens to the Slaughter House and on both sides of the humpbacked Grand Canal. And he haunted the little square of blessed memory where he had once carried her across the wet water, chain smoking used butts from a pocketful in his overcoat as he watched a steam-breathed sweeper sweeping at the mud with a twig broom; but she never appeared. A few of his former clients passed by, all ignoring him but the large aristocratic lady, who called him a son-of-a-dog-in-heat. You can't win them all.

Afterwards, wandering along the Mercerie in the early evening, through a shop window hung with wires dripping strings of glass beads and trinkets, he had the sudden sense he had glimpsed her, saw himself reflected in her large dark eyes. If he was truly conscious she was standing behind a counter, this slim-bodied, slant-eyed, long-nosed, handsome Venetian, staring at him as though contemplating the mark of fate in the face of a stranger. Then taking another swift look and this time recognizing who he was she lifted a frightened hand to her bosom and turned abruptly away. He ducked close to the glass under the beads, pawing the window as though to see her better, but she was no longer there; the shop was empty. Fidelman flung away a good butt and entered. The shop was crowded, its shelves laden with glass knicknacks, baubles, Madonnas, medallions, crap for tourists, which proved nothing although he wondered if she had disappeared for reasons of taste.

Where the woman had been, now stood a near-sighted man past sixty, in a grey suit, with puffy brows and pot-belly, who gazed at the former ferryman in surprise, if not distaste – as though he knew he was there for no good cause – yet courteously inquired if he could assist him. Fidelman, secretly shivering, modestly priced a vase or two, politely listened to the verdict, nodded, bowed, casting a wild look through the open door into the rear room where a corpulent glass blower sat at a table working with a small torch, in the process of creating a green glass snake; but no one else. After desperately trying to think what else to do, pretending to be thoughtfully counting the change in his pocket though they both knew he had none, then asking if he could use the gabinetto and being refused, Fidelman thanked the shopkeeper and left. He had visions of her disappearing in a mist. The next day, and every day for two weeks thereafter he passed the shop seven or eight times daily. The shopkeeper once in exasperation thrust his arm at him in an obscene gesture but otherwise paid no attention. Fidelman never saw his dream girl in the shop. He had doubts he ever had: trompe l'oeil, mirage, déjà vue, or something of the sort.

He then gave her up, no easy trick if you had nothing. Like blowing kisses or kissing blows. Eh, Fidelman, you old cocker, there was a time you would have held on longer. On to what? I had nothing, I gave up nothing. Nothing from nothing equals nothing. Say more and it's confronting death. On the other hand spring came early that year; to his surprise flowers looking out of house windows. Young jewel-like leaves of myrtles and laurels rose above ancient brick walls in back alleys. Subtle pinks, apricots, lavenders streaked an underwater architecture of floating Gothic and Moorish palazzi. Mosaics glittered, golden and black, on the faces of churches. Sandali sailed under bridges, heaped high with eggplants, green peppers, mounds of string beans. The canals widened, golden light on green water, pure Canaletto all the way to the Rialto. A sense of sea enlivened the air, lagoon and Adriatic under high blue sky above the outer islands. Fantasticando: Eastern galleons, huge battle-tubs approaching with cannons booming, star and crescent billowing on red sails, from Byzantium of mosaic saints and dancing dolphins. Boom, tara, War! History, the Most Serene Venetian Republic, Othello singing Verdi as Desdemona tussles in the hay with Iago under a weeping-willow tree. Fidelman, golden-robed Doge of Venice, though maybe better not since they garrotted, stabbed, poisoned half the poor bastards. The Doge is dead, long live the dog that did him in! Boom, tara, yay! Fidelman III, Crusader on horse, hacking at Saladin and a thousand infidels! Fidelman in the Accademia! Ah Bellini, Giorgione, Tiziano, carissimi! The ex-painter wiped a wet eyelid, felt better and decided he hadn't given her up after all. She is still present, lives in the mind. He kept an eye cocked for the sight of her, and with surprise, though not astonishment spied her in the glass trinket shop, which he now passed only once in a longing while. There she wasn't but if you looked again, she was.

Churchbells.

Cannon scattering pigeons in San Marco.

Gondolas lit with Japanese lanterns.

Holy Mother, you have sent your Blessed Daughter. His heart, if he had a bit left, missed six beats and flapped like a mass of furled banners. He tapped on the window and out she came.

They talked quickly, intensely, searching one another with six eyes. She spoke her name: Margherita Fassoli, that made it real, an immediate commitment. She was herself real at last, no longer wildgoose shade he chased in a maze of dead-end canals, under low arches, and in alleyways. Breathless, she had only a moment; her uncle out for an espresso forbade her to be friendly with strangers. She had been ill for weeks – niente, a persistent virus – was better now, had hoped he would come by. He did not say how often he had, fruitlessly.

'Fidelman,' he told her. 'Where can we go, I have no money?'

She seemed momentarily stunned, hadn't given it a thought; then confessed she was a married woman – he knew – her husband a glass blower who worked in Murano, Beppo Fassoli. If nothing else he treated her kindly. 'He gets annoyed about the kids sometimes but otherwise he's considerate. I'm sure you'll like him, he's wise about life.'

'I can't invite you to my dump, Margherita,' Fidelman said. 'All it is is a lousy rathole with a bed that would collapse with two in it. And nothing else but a wine bottle to piss in. Should you open the window you have no idea of the stench of the canal.'

She was desolated, squeezed her hands white but could not offer her place. They had four rooms and two boys, Riccardo and Rodolfo, eight and ten, little terrors. That made her around thirty or so, not a bad age for a woman. She was simple, spontaneous, direct – had already taken his hard hand and pressed it to her bosom. Her nose and eyes, pure Venetian. Her glossy hair, parted in the centre, was rolled in braided circles over the ears. Her eyes were beyond him: the depth, light in dark, quiet enduring sadness – who knows where or from what. Whoever she was she knew who.

Margherita was urging him to go before her uncle returned.

'I will if you say when I can see you.'

She gazed at him hungrily, eating with mouth, eyes. 'Do you really want to, caro? There are so many better-looking women around.'

'Passionately. But it's now or never, I'm frankly famished. Another day of dreaming and I'm a dead man. The ghost gives up.'

'Oh my God, what do you mean?'

'I mean living on dreams. Sleeping with them. I can't any more though I've accomplished nothing.'

'Mio caro,' she all but wept.

'Couldn't we go some place you know? I haven't a lousy

lira to rent a room. Do you happen to have a friend with an apartment we could borrow?'

She reflected hopelessly. Though her eyes lit she shrugged her shoulders.

'Maybe. I'll have to ask. But stop shivering as though you were in heat and take your hand out of your pocket. It doesn't look nice.'

'I won't apologize for my passion. I'm hard up, it's now or never.'

She finally agreed, asked him to meet her at the campanile after work. She would beg off around three.

'The boys come home from school at six and I've got to be there or they'll wreck the furniture. Beppo doesn't control them well enough. Usually he's not home before eight.'

'All we need is a good hour.'

'There's no need to rush, caro.'

They kissed in the street. A passing tourist snapped a picture. The uncle hurried towards them, nearsightedly seeing nothing. Margherita disappeared into the shop as Fidelman walked quickly way.

This time is different, this one loves me.

They met at the bell tower, a dozen clucking pigeons at their feet. Margherita was tired around the eyes, a smudge of darkness, but worked up a listless smile; he blamed it on her recent illness. On the walk across the neck of the city she became animated again, showed him where Tintoretto had lived, in a Moorish section with turbaned figures and kneeling camels sculptured on stone plaques on house walls. Her matchstick street, take a few steps you were out of it, led into Fondamenta Nuove. In fact from her door he could see the island cemetery, thick with graves, across the water. They entered an old building, scabby masonry showing thin orange bricks, four storeys high, terrazzi at the top floor loaded with potted plants – this house separated from the one it leaned towards across the narrow way by two or three buttresses at rooftop. She walked up the stairs, Fidelman at her direction trailing by two flights. He heard her open three locks with a bunch of keys. She left the door ajar for him.

'I'll undress, you come in after I'm in bed,' she said.

'Wouldn't you want me to undress you?'

'I'm a modest person. I can't help it, don't press me.'

But Fidelman, after quickly counting to a hundred and fifty, walked in on her anyway. She was standing in the semi-dark, the blinds down, but he found the light and snapped it on.

'You couldn't wait,' she said bitterly.

'Painters love nudes, also ex-painters.'

She was patient as he looked her over: heavier in the haunch and breasts than he had imagined; these were strong binding garments she wore. Her shapely legs were veined, splotched purple here and there. Slim at the waist but the stomach streaked with lesions of her pregnancies. She was forty if she was a day.

'Well, caro, are you disenchanted?'

'No more than usual,' Fidelman confessed. 'Still, you're not bad-looking although you play yourself down.'

'At my age there's no pretending I'm in the first flush of youth.'

She unbraided her hair. They sank into a deep bed with high head- and foot-board and at once embraced.

'Why you're not hard at all,' she said in surprise. He removed his member from her hand. 'I'll get there myself, it won't take but a few minutes. Just act affectionate.'

Her breasts were formless and he felt a roll of flesh above

158

her hips. Fidelman snapped on the lamp. The same woman. He snapped it off.

'Do you mind if I get on top?' she asked. 'It's hard to breathe since I had my illness.'

'Be my guest.'

They were tender to each other and both soon came, Margherita with vigour, making sounds of pleasure, Fidelman a while after in thoughtful silence. He fell asleep for a few minutes, had a quick dream which he couldn't recall. When he woke the blinds were up, Margherita filing her nails in bed. An old woman in a padded chair at the window was reading a folded newspaper.

The ex-painter sat up. 'For Christ's sake, who is she?'

'Beppo's mother. She likes to read at that window. Don't worry, she won't say a thing. She's a deaf-mute in both ears.'

'My God, she can write, can't she?'

'Don't get excited, she's not a suspicious type. I called a friend as you asked me to, but she couldn't accommodate us. I don't care for her sort anyway, she gives herself airs, so it's just as well. That's why I brought you here. Are you disappointed, amore mio?'

Beppo Fassoli, when Fidelman arrived one night famished for supper – he now supported himself by hawking corn for pigeons on the Piazza San Marco – gave his guest a glass rose with six red petals. The radio was blaring Cavaradossi singing, 'L'arte nel suo mistero/ Le diverse bellezze insiem confonde –' but Beppo snapped it off impatiently.

'The red in this rose is Venetian red. It is made from twenty-four-carat gold mixed in the formula.'

'Real gold? You don't say.' The ex-painter, touched by

the gift, was embarrassed at being given since he had already taken.

'What do you make besides roses?'

The glass blower shrugged. 'Fish, flasks of all sorts, the sentimental animals of Disney. Our craft has fallen to the level of the taste of the tourists.'

'Eh,' Fidelman agreed.

Margherita sat at the head of the table, ladling out plates of steaming ravioli to Rodolfo and Riccardo, quiet only while eating: otherwise slapping, kicking, shoving, incessantly testing each other's strength of arm, leg, lung. Beppo's old mother sat at the other end of the table attending her son at her right hand, Fidelman opposite him feeling terribly exposed. The deaf woman was up and down to supply the glass blower with ravioli, cheese, bread, white wine; she counted spoonfuls of sugar into his espresso, stirred the cup and sipped a taste before he drank. Beppo ate slowly, paying little attention to his wife. He never once addressed her, except to throw her a look, with drawn thick brows – his eyes were green – when the boys were getting restless. She shut them up with a hiss and a glare. In that case, concluded Fidelman, nobody's cuckolding anybody. Beppo moodily picked his teeth with a fork tine. Their eyes met across two empty ravioli plates and both gazed away.

Though short of inches, the glass blower was a strong, muscular, handsome type, thick-shouldered, hairy. He appeared younger than his wife but Fidelman knew he wasn't. Maybe she looked older because he looked younger, an easy way to slap her in the face. If he was slapping; Fidelman wasn't sure. Did Beppo suspect him of usurping his rights as husband? Had the old deaf mother spelled it out on paper; she did not, after all, see with her ears, suspicious or not. He worried but Margherita assured him it was a waste of time.

'He doesn't know, just keep calm.'

'He won't find out? I'd hate to hurt him – or vice versa. Mightn't he guess, do you think?'

'It's not his nature. His mind is usually occupied with other matters. There are men of that sort.'

'What occupies his mind?'

'Everything but me. On the other hand it's full of facts and fantasy. He also likes to live life. His father was the same but died young.'

Beppo seemed to like the ex-painter's company. He liked, he said, the artistic viewpoint. Once he rowed Fidelman to Murano to see the glass factory where he worked, VETRERIE ARTISTICHE. While they were there he blew Fidelman a small bird and set it in the cooling oven. The next night he presented it to him at supper to the applause of all at the table. He also invited the guest to go rowing in the lagoon Sunday with him and the boys. Beppo fished and caught nothing. The ex-painter, never having caught anything in his life, would not fish; he had vague thoughts of sketching but hadn't brought along pad or pencil. Fidelman enjoyed watching the floating city from the water. Venice, sober, dark, sank in winter; rose, a magic island giving off light, in summer. They rowed behind the Giudecca, the boys diving naked off the boat, their young asses flashing in sunlight before they splashed into blue water.

'Bravi, ragazzi,' Beppo cheered. 'Bello! Bellissimo! Non è bello, Fidelman?'

'Beautiful,' murmured Fidelman, without innocence. He was spending more and more time with the glass blower, though it wasn't exactly easy to be sleeping with a man's wife and being friends with him. Still, somebody else might have made an effort to dislike him. Fidelman now visited Margherita one or two afternoons a week, depending on circumstances and desire – mostly hers; he was experiencing the first long liaison of his life. And he stayed often for supper because Beppo made it a standing invitation.

'I'm ashamed to leech on you.'

'What's an extra plate of macaroni?'

He thought of Margherita's sex as an extra plate of something.

After supper they left the kids and dishes to the women. Beppo knew the cafés and liked the one the gondoliers frequented in Calle degli Assassini – away from the tourists, who had their own way of drowning the city. They drank grappa, played cards, sang and told each other the day's adventures. When they were bored they watched television. The ex-painter, a butt in his mouth, liked to sketch the gondoliers in all poses and positions. When Beppo complimented him on one or two of the drawings, Fidelman confided to him the failures of his life in art. The glass blower listened at length with moody tender interest. It made Fidelman increasingly unhappy to be sleeping with Margherita and confessing irrelevancies to her husband; but the more he thought about it the more convinced he became that Beppo knew the situation and tolerated it. Is it because we're friends and he likes me? he asked himself, but then figured the man had a girl of his own somewhere, possibly Murano.

One day the glass blower confessed he slept with his wife on rare occasions, including her birthdays.

'Doesn't that make it hard all around?' the ex-painter asked thickly.

'Some things are harder than others.'

Relieved of guilt, Fidelman all but embraced him.

That night, in a burst of inspiration and trust, he asked Beppo to come to his room on Sunday morning to look at his paintings – the few that remained. He had destroyed most but had kept a dozen perhaps justificatory pictures, and a few pieces of sculpture.

'I'll give you a private exhibition.' He did not ask himself why; he was afraid of the answer.

'Do you like art, Beppo?'

'I love art,' said the glass blower. 'It comes to me naturally.'

'What does?'

'Love for art. I never studied it at school. My taste formed itself naturally.'

'This isn't classic stuff, if you know what I mean. It's modernist and you mightn't care for it.'

Beppo answered that he had attended the last five Biennali. 'My spirit is modern,' he said haughtily.

'I was only kidding,' Fidelman answered lamely, but the truth of it was he was no longer eager to show the glass blower his work and didn't know how to withdraw with grace, without insulting him more than he already might have.

Sunday morning, in a panic at his folly, he ran to Beppo's flat to tell him not to come, but Margherita, half-dressed, said he had already left. She invited Fidelman to stay for a half hour, the boys were in church; but the ex-painter was running with all his might and beat Beppo to his house. He seriously considered flight, hiding, not answering the bell; then Beppo knocked and entered, wincing at the disorder.

Fidelman apologized: he had changed his mind. 'If you didn't like my paintings it'd make me feel bad, especially since you're a dear friend.'

'I understand, Arturo, but maybe it's better to show me

163

your work anyway. Who knows, I might be genuinely enthusiastic. Besides, if we're friends, we're friends for good or bad, better or worse.'

Fidelman, touched, confused, not at all sure he knew what he was doing, or why, lifted a canvas and placed it on the kitchen table, against the wall, facing a small round window.

'This, you'll notice, has been influenced by Barney Newman, if you know who he is. The broad lavender band bisecting the black field at dead centre is obviously the vital element organizing the picture. At the same time it achieves, partly through colour, a quality of linear universality, in my case horizontal whereas Newman does it vertically. Lately I've been sort of thinking maybe I could paint something more original based on a series of criss-crossing abstract canals.'

Beppo nodded gravely. Leaning forward in somewhat the pose of Rodin's Thinker with a bit of belly, he sat on a half barrel Fidelman had in his room for want of a chair, his broad feet placed apart, his trousers hiked up his hairy shins and calves, an unlit long cigar in his mouth. He gazed at the picture as if he were seeing it forever, with a shade of puzzlement and annoyance Fidelman noted and feared: half-stunned if it weren't concentration – and occasionally Beppo sighed. It occurred to the ex-painter that he looked in his handsome way much like his mother. Who is this man? he thought, and why am I breaking my heart for him: I mean do I have to show him my private work? Why the revelation? He had then and there an urge to paint Beppo to his core, so much like a seizure he thought of it as sexual, and to his surprise found himself desiring Margherita so strongly he had to restrain himself from rushing out to jump into bed with her.

My life will end in calamity, Fidelman thought. Everything is out of joint again and I'm not helping by showing these pictures. You can pull up nails and let the past loose once too often.

Reluctantly, as if he were lifting pure lead, he placed a framed painting on the table.

'This is a spray job, an undercoating of apple-green acrylic resin, then a haphazard haze of indigo, creating a mood and a half before I applied a reconciling rose in varying values and intensities. Note how the base colours, invading without being totally visible, infect the rose so that it's both present and you might say evanescing. It's hard to explain a picture of this sort because it's something more than merely a poem of colour. We're dealing with certain kinds of essences. In a way this and the other picture I just showed you are related, the other stating the masculine principle, this obviously feminine. Frankly, the inspiration is Rothko but I learned a trick or two from some of the things I've seen in *Art News* done by my contemporaries.'

His voice at this point cracked, but Beppo's expression was unchanged and he still said nothing.

A scow passing by in the canal below agitated gem-like reflections of sunlit water on the ceiling. Fidelman waited till the rumble of the boat had disappeared into the distance.

'This,' he said wearily, 'is an old sculpture I did years ago, "Fragment of a Head" – marble.'

Beppo, as though smiling, nodded.

A broken head he responds to. Jesus God, whatever led me to do this? It'll all end in disaster.

In quick succession he showed a surrealistic landscape based on a frottage of tree bark, an old still life with rotting flowers, an old madonna with old child, and an old sentimental self-portrait.

'These show me at various phases of development,' Fidelman said, barely able to speak. 'You needn't comment on each if you don't want to, though I would be interested in your overall impression.'

Beppo sat silent, lighting his cigar.

'Here's a piece of pop sculpture, "Soft Toilet Seat", made out of vinylite. It was exhibited for two weeks in New York City. Originally I had a triptych of seats nailed on beaverboard more or less saying, 'Fuck all art, one must be free of the artistic alibi', though I don't wholly subscribe to that. I can just take so much dada, so I cut it down to the single seat you see before you.'

'Can you shit through it?' the glass blower ultimately asked.

'Art isn't life,' Fidelman said. Then he said, 'Don't be a wise guy, Beppo.'

'Not that these things can't be done but you haven't done them. Your work lacks authority and originality. It lacks more than that, but I won't say what now. If you want my advice there's one thing I'd do with this stuff.'

'Such as what?' said the ex-painter, fearing the worst.

'Burn them all.'

'I thought you'd say that, you cruel fairy bastard.'

Leaping up with Fidelman's kitchen knife in his hand, Beppo slashed the toilet seat and two paintings.

Fidelman interposed his body between the knife and the other canvasses. 'Have mercy!'

'Let me finish these off,' the glass blower said hoarsely. 'It's for your own sake. Show who's master of your fate – bad art or you.'

Fidelman savagely struggled with him for the knife but

166

at a crucial moment, as though a spinning colour wheel had turned dead white, something failed in him and he relaxed his grip. Beppo quickly slashed up the other canvasses. Afterwards they went downstairs and in a corner of the junk-filled vegetable patch next to the smelly back canal, burned everything, including the fragmented marble head, which Beppo had smashed against a rock.

'Don't waste your life doing what you can't do.'

'Why shouldn't I keep trying?'

'After twenty years if the rooster hasn't crowed she should know she's a hen. Your painting will never pay back the part of your life you've given up for it.'

'What about Van Gogh? He never sold a single painting in his lifetime.'

'You're not Van Gogh. Besides he was crazy.'

Fidelman left the garden in a stupor; he wandered a day, his eyes glazed in grief. On Tuesday, somewhat calmer through exhaustion, though the weight of his emptiness dragged like a dead dog chained around his neck, he presented himself to Margherita, who, with tears in her eyes, embraced him, knowing what had happened.

'Come, tesoro,' she said, leading him to the marriage bed. 'For our mutual relief, me from my life and you from art.'

As they were in the midst of violent intercourse, Fidelman on top, Margherita more loving than ever, the bedroom door opened and he glimpsed a nude hairy body wearing a horn or carrying a weapon; before he could rise he felt Beppo land on him. Fidelman cried out, expecting death between the shoulders. Margherita, shoving herself up with a grunt, slipped out from under them and fled out of the room. Fidelman rolled to the right and left to be rid of his incubus, but Beppo had him tightly pinned, his nose to the bedboard, his ass in the air.

'Don't hurt me, Beppo, please, I have piles.'

'It'll be a cool job, I'm wearing mentholated vaseline. You'll be surprised at the pleasure.'

'Is your mother watching?'

'At her age she has no curiosity.'

'I suppose I deserve this.'

'Think of love,' the glass blower murmured. 'You've run from it all your life.'

He stopped running.

Venice slowed down though it went on floating, its canals floating on Venice.

'Leonardo, Michelangelo,' Fidelman murmured.

'If you can't invent art, invent life,' Beppo advised him.

For good or ill Fidelman loved him; he could not help himself; he ought to have known. Beppo was handsome, hardworking, and loved to breathe; he smelled (and tasted) of oil and vineagar; he was, after all, a tender man and gentle lover. Fidelman had never in his life said 'I love you' without reservation to anyone. He said it to Beppo. If that's the way it works, that's the way it works. Better love than not love. If you sneeze at life it backs off and instead of fruit you're holding a bone. If I'm a late bloomer at least I've bloomed in love.

'It's a good way to be,' explained Beppo, 'we're not like everybody else. I like it better with men because the company is more interesting and it's easier to be friends with somebody who speaks your language.'

They were together as often as possible, everywhere except in Beppo's house. Fidelman had stopped going there.

'Naturally,' said Beppo. 'It wouldn't be discreet.'

'What does Margherita say?'

'She's said it before, I don't listen.'

'Will you stay married to her?'

'Of course. I've got two boys and an old mother to think of.'

'I guess so,' said Fidelman.

Yet he was for once in his life on the whole serene; discontented only during the day when they were on separate islands, Beppo in Murano, and Fidelman selling pigeon feed on the Piazza San Marco. He spent most of his time thinking of Beppo and the glass blower said he thought of him. They talked it over and one summer morning Fidelman gave up his bird-food business and went with Beppo to Murano. At 6 a.m. they met at the Fondamenta Nuove. They stepped into Beppo's rowboat, and each taking an oar, rowed past San Michele towards Murano. The water was calm and it took no more than twenty minutes to reach the island. Beppo spoke quietly to the assistant manager of the glassworks and got him to put on his friend as an apprentice and part-time man of all work. He was the oldest of the apprentices, some of them kids, but he didn't mind because Beppo, who was teaching him the rites of love, also taught him to blow glass.

Working with the hot molten glass excited Fidelman sexually. He felt creative, his heart in his pants. 'With pipe, tongs, shears, you can make a form or change it into its opposite,' Beppo said. 'For instance, with a snip or two of the scissors, if it suits you, you can change the male organ into the female.' The glass blower laughed heartily. Fidelman doubted he would be so minded; the thought evoked pain. Still it helped you understand the possibilities of life. And amid the possibilities was working with glass as an art form, though for certain reasons he did not say say so to Beppo, who all day long, his face wet, armpits sweated, at intervals swigging from a beer or water bottle, blew varieties of fish and Disney creatures served up to him by an assistant from a wood or steel mould, for further shaping and decoration. For a change of pace he blew wine goblets, slim-waisted vases, flasks of odd shapes and sizes.

Fidelman, among other things, loved dipping the tapered blowpipe into the flaming opening of the noisy furnace -- like poking into the living substance of the sun for a puddle of flowing fire -- Prometheus Fidelman -- a viscous gob of sunflesh hanging from the pipe like a human organ: breast, kidney, stomach or phallus, cooling as it gaseously flamed, out of which if one were skilled enough, lucky, knew the right people, he would create glass objects of expected yet unexpected forms. He blew gently into the red-hot glowing mass a single soft bubble of breath -- it made no difference if the blower had eaten garlic or flowers -- a small inside hole without spittle or seeds, a teardrop, gut, uterus, which itself became its object of birth: a sculptured womb; shaped, elongated by pendulum swing of pipe, the living metal teased and shorn into shape by tongs and scissors. Give the bubble a mouth and it became beaker, ewer, vase, amphora or burial urn, anything the mouth foretold, or heart desired, or blower could blow. If you knew how, you could blow anything.

Not yet of course Fidelman although he was learning. As apprentice he blew as Beppo shaped; or delivered the master fresh fish, Birds of Paradise, woodland creatures that he or another assistant blew into pristine form in moulds; he also applied stems to vessels blown by Beppo, the stem shaped by a flick or two of his tool. To permit him to open and work at the mouth of any kind of container, Fidelman aimed a red-hot cone of glass at the bubble's bottom, Beppo gripping the gob with his tongs and leading it to the point of attachment. With his shears he creased the neck of the bubble and with a tap detached it from the blowpipe; he left Fidelman holding the open-mouthed possibility: the open mouth. Every move they made was in essence sexual, a marvellous interaction because, among other things, it saved time and trouble: you worked and loved at once. When a glass object was completed, Fidelman hastily trotted to the cooling kiln in the rear with the thing on a wooden board, to stash away before it cracked. And he handed one tool or another to Beppo, who hardly looked at him during working hours, the assistant assisting for love's sake however he could. There were no spoken orders once you knew the process. He watched the glass blower and foresaw his needs, in essence a new experience for him. Otherwise he stood by, greedily watching the masters at other benches to absorb what they knew.

Impatient, agitated at times by all there was to learn, the variety of skills to master, Fidelman persuaded Beppo to stay on and teach him for an hour or two after the crowd of glass workers had gone home, the workshop talk and shouting silenced, five of the six furnace openings banked down, one blazing in a perpetual violet and lemon roar. He practised then what he couldn't during the day, and though Beppo, eating an apple or smoking a butt, did not always encourage it, blew forms he had never blown before, or seen blown, evolving monstrosities of glass, so huge and complicated it took fifteen minutes to break their grip on the iron when he wanted to discard them. Many of Fidelman's creations cracked in mid-air, or against something on the workbench in a careless move. Those he completed intact stood (or fell) unbalanced, lopsided, malformed. But he worked for the first time in his life, instructed. Up to now he had taught himself and not got over it.

In the fall Margherita objected to the nightwork – it

was killing her husband. Beppo's complexion had turned pale, his eyes were bloodshot, the skin around them, dark and puffy. She was already half a widow, what more did they want? Abandoning the night sessions they came to work earlier, at half past four, leaving the Fondamenta bundled in overcoats against the stabbing wet cold, the fog cradled on the choppy water plopping against the boats at the dock, a star visible if they were lucky. They navigated by instinct – Beppo's – and made Murano usually on time, though once in a while they rowed in circles around the cemetery, lost in and breathing fog. 'In the end we pay for everything,' Beppo muttered. Suffering from loss of sleep he sometimes conked out at his work during the day, Fidelman having to wake him furtively; so in the end they decided that the apprentice himself would stay on alone nights, doing what he felt he had to do. Each assured the other it was for his benefit. 'Though in a way it's mad,' said the master to Fidelman; 'the more you give up the more you undertake.'

However it was arranged and settled with the assistant manager, who had been assured it was all for the good of the company. Because Beppo left in the rowboat, and the vaporetto, before it expired at midnight, was fantastically slow making its stations, Fidelman considered renting a second-hand rowboat for himself; but then the thought occurred that taking a small room in a house on Murano, maybe with a little garden, would make more sense – be cheaper in the long run, and he could spend more time in the factory. Beppo could stay over when he felt like it, and they would as usual be together on Sundays.

Fidelman located a tiny room on Campo S. Bernardo, from which he could see the airport on the mainland and Burano and Torcello. But Beppo, when he heard, was infuriated. 'You have no consideration for others, it's plain to see.'

After he had calmed down, he said, 'Why are you so fanatic about this accursed glass? After all, it's only glass.'

'Life is short if you don't hurry.'

'A fanatic never knows when to stop. It's obvious you want to repeat your fate.'

'What fate do you have in mind?'

'Yours.'

The apprentice sighed but hurried. For months he tried everything he saw others doing: cut glass in diamond patterns, carved glass as gems, practised diamond point and acid engraving, flash painting with stains, gold and silver leaf applied in reverse: gods and goddesses in classic poses pretending left is right. In the spring he hungered to be involved with modern forms. Fidelman envisioned glass sculptures, a difficult enterprise, deciding first to experiment with compositions of mixed colours ladelled into and cast in moulds. He invented objets trouvés – what better way to find what wasn't lost? – and worked with peacock's tails and Argus eyes in targets, casting concentric circles: amber/ lavender/ black/ green. He fabricated abstract stained-glass windows, created Op Art designs of mosaics, collages of broken glass, and spent hours dripping glass on hot glass in the manner of Pollock.

Beppo from time to time watched, picking his teeth with an old toothpick.

'You're doing the same things you did in your paintings, that's the lousy hair in the egg. It's easy to see, half a talent is worse than none.'

His criticism upset Fidelman so badly that he did not appear in the factory for a week. Is he wrong or am I? He went back one night to see what he had done, and when

173

he saw, chopped it up with a hammer. He decided again, as he had more than once in the past, that he had no true distinction as an artist and this time would try not to forget it.

Fidelman cut out night work and spent the time with Beppo in the city. The glass blower asked no questions and made no comments. He was once again very tender and after a while Fidelman's heart stopped being a brick and began breathing. They drank with the gondoliers on the Calle degli Assassini and stayed away from painters and sculptors.

One day when they met by accident on the Rialto, Margherita, her large eyes vague, hair plaited in circles over her ears, her arms around a grocery bundle, stopped Fidelman and begged him to leave Venice.

'Listen, Fidelman, we've been friends, let's stay friends. All I ask is that you leave Beppo and go some place else. After all, in the eyes of God he's my husband. Now, because of you he's rarely around and my family is a mess. The boys are always in trouble, his mother complains all day, and I'm at the end of my strength. Beppo may be a homo but he's a good provider and not a bad father when there are no men friends around to divert him from domestic life. The boys listen to his voice when they hear it. We have our little pleasures. He knows life and keeps me informed. Sometimes we visit friends, sometimes we go to a movie together and stop at a bar on our way home. In other words, things are better when he's around even though the sex is short. Occasionally he will throw me a lay if I suck him up good beforehand. It isn't a perfect life but I've learned to be satisfied, and was, more or less, before you came around. Since then, though there was some pleasure with you – I don't deny it – it ended quickly, and to tell the truth I'm worse off than I was before, so that's why I ask you to go.'

In despair Fidelman rowed back to the factory and blew a huge glass bubble, larger and thicker than any he had blown before. He got it off the blowpipe with the help of an apprentice he had persuaded to stay over, and worked on its mouth in fear and doubtful confidence with tongs and a wet opening tool of smoking wood. Heating and re-heating for several nights, he dipped, swung, lengthened, shaped, until the glass on his blowpipe turned out to be a capacious heavy red bowl, iron become ice. When he had cooled it without cracking he considered etching on it some scenes of Venice but decided no. The bowl was severe and graceful and sat solid, upright. It held the clear light and even seemed to listen. Fidelman polished it carefully, and when it was done, filled it with cold water and with a sigh dipped in his hands. He showed the bowl to Beppo, who said it was a good job, beautifully proportioned and reminding him of something the old Greeks had done. I kept my finger in art, Fidelman wept when he was alone. The next day, though they searched high and low with a crowd of apprentices, the bowl was missing and could not be found. Beppo suspected the assistant manager.

Before leaving Venice, Fidelman blew a slightly hump-backed green horse for Beppo, the colour of his eyes. 'Up yours,' said the glass blower, grieving at the grey in Fidelman's hair. He sold the horse for a decent sum and gave Fidelman the lire. They kissed and parted.

Fidelman sailed from Venice on a Portuguese freighter.

In America he worked as a craftsman in glass and loved men and women.

THE HISTORY OF VINTAGE

The famous American publisher Alfred A. Knopf (1892–1984) founded Vintage Books in the United States in 1954 as a paperback home for the authors published by his company. Vintage was launched in the United Kingdom in 1990 and works independently from the American imprint although both are part of the international publishing group, Random House.

Vintage in the United Kingdom was initially created to publish paperback editions of books bought by the prestigious literary hardback imprints in the Random House Group such as Jonathan Cape, Chatto & Windus, Hutchinson and later William Heinemann, Secker & Warburg and The Harvill Press. There are many Booker and Nobel Prize-winning authors on the Vintage list and the imprint publishes a huge variety of fiction and non-fiction. Over the years Vintage has expanded and the list now includes great authors of the past – who are published under the Vintage Classics imprint – as well as many of the most influential authors of the present. In 2012 Vintage Children's Classics was launched to include the much-loved authors of our youth.

For a full list of the books Vintage publishes, please visit our website www.vintage-books.co.uk

For book details and other information about the classic authors we publish, please visit the Vintage Classics website www.vintage-classics.info

www.vintage-classics.info

**Visit www.worldofstories.co.uk for all your
favourite children's classics**